Notice

All characters, place , ...

fictitious and are not associated or inspired by

any person, living or dead. The author was not

striving for historical or geographical accuracy as

all places and events are purely fictional and not

intended to be accurate.

License Notes

CORINNE LEIGH
DONOVAN

A MIND
ABDUCTED

To my husband and three children. You are my world. I love you and I am so blessed.

Contents:

1

The crisp November wind chilled my fingertips as I tightened the oversized hoodie around my face. I held my tongue out to the sky, plucking the falling snowflakes from the cold, dense air as Mom put Em down for a nap.

There was no sound but the crunch of grass beneath my feet. Tomorrow is my 13th birthday, but I'm not expecting much. I know better. Mom and Eric have fallen on hard times. It's one of those things kids don't understand, or so I'm told.

I learned early on not to ask too many questions. The mail comprised of countless yellow and pink envelopes. That alone was enough to keep me quiet.

I moved on from the snowflakes, noticing the slick driveway before me. I coasted from one end to the other, grappling my arm around the light post, pivoting myself around and back again.

The ominous sky darkened, but it was not yet evening. In the dreary, cold darkness, I shivered. The wind whipped through the trees; the remaining leaves dove as if hiding from the fierce cold. I ducked into the porch to avoid the cutting chill.

A fire truck siren squealed in the distance as a car drove by, then another and another. After blowing warm breath onto my fingertips, I hopped off the porch and spun in circles with my head held back and arms outstretched, mouth open, taking in the cold snow. The peace I felt wouldn't last long. I shuffled my feet, slip 'n sliding across the driveway, forming tracks in the light, powdery snow.

The unmistakable sound of Eric's Chevy rumbled from a distance. I picked up speed and slid across the driveway and back to the porch as he whipped over the curb, clipping the garbage cans before coming to a stop. Ducking into the shadows, I spied Eric's angry demeanor as he slammed the Blazer door with force, failing to notice my presence. While he leaned over the car, he mumbled to himself as his thumb and middle finger massaged his temples.

I escaped into the house. Awaiting my punishment for tracking in the wet, sloshy snow, I cringed. Mom briefly looked up from drawing large red circles on the newspaper. Feeling invisible, I mentioned wanting tacos for dinner, almost hoping she'd notice my tracks so her focus would turn to me. She nodded as she drew her eyes back to the paper.

My lungs filled as I closed my eyes, willing myself to stay silent. Somehow, I knew that I should leave them in private. Em was still napping, so coloring seemed to be the best activity for the time being.

I colored, alone with my thoughts, hearing only Em's rhythmic breathing and the creaking of the house; the wind punished the rattling windowpanes with its brute force.

The door slammed. A long dark line of Jazzberry Jam inspired color jutted beyond the edge of the page as I jumped at the noise of the heavy door. I heard the heavy boots hit the doorframe from being thrown in anger. Em stirred and I hushed her back to sleep.

With my ear pressed against my bedroom door, I held my breath. They began using words I'm not allowed to say. His voice raised an octave as Mom dissolved in tears.

She yelled, her voice shaking, yet firm, "You have to stop and think! Don't you get it? We're drowning here! It's the third time in six months you've been under review!"

His maddening voice bellowed, "Angie, don't you think I know that?" His clattering feet paced the kitchen. "I don't see you making any changes! For just once, I wish you could be in my shoes. I am working my ass to the bone at the freighter for you and those kids!"

With a tone of regret, she answered, "You made me believe in you—made me believe this is what you wanted! Those kids are everything to me so if you're out, then GET OUT!"

One moment later, I heard the door as Eric stormed out again.

I rushed to Em's side as she continued to stir. I held her tight, not knowing if I was subduing her fears or my own. Through it all, I heard Mom's muffled sobs.

***

Her shadow blocked the light at the base of my door. I pictured her hesitating, taking a deep breath with her hand on the doorknob. The door opened and red, swollen eyes peered in.

I asked with hesitation, "Did he get fired?"

"No, Josie, he just had a rough day."

I knew that was a half-truth, but I didn't press her.

Tears began to emerge. Unsure whether they were tears of relief, fear, or longing, I turned my back to her and allowed them to spill over my cheeks. I longed for things to be happy again. Eric had never been the most loving father figure, but things were okay. I was no longer angry with my dad for leaving, but secretly still awaited his return. I wanted to tell my mom that things would be different if Dad was here, but I remained silent.

"Come on, it's time to set the table for dinner," she said as she made her way to Em's crib.

The savory smell of chicken potpie engulfed my room as I swung the door open. It wasn't tacos, but it would do. Mom was trying to make everything seem normal, and chicken potpie was comforting, the best we could ask for when needing normalcy. Em reached out as Mom pulled her from the crib. I stood, waiting for Mom to say more. I looked at her as she turned from Em's crib and headed for the door. I followed her, shuffling my feet as I made my way to the kitchen.

We sat down to dinner. Em was playing in her potpie as Mom and I stared ahead. I lifted the top layer of my potpie to allow steam to escape. I looked up to see the wavy image of my Mom beyond the hot steam's path.

I broke the silence, "Mom?"

"Hmm," she answered.

"If he didn't get fired, why are you fighting?"

She looked at me with sad eyes and with her hand placed over mine said, "Josie, it's something you'll understand someday. He has troubles—grown-up troubles. There are things he does that you don't understand yet. He is under a lot of pressure providing for our family."

"Oh," was all I could muster.

I had more questions. I remembered what I heard Mom say to Eric, *You have to stop and think!* I wondered to myself what Mom was talking about. Did he get in trouble? Did he get in a fight? What is going on?

Dinner ended in silence. After clearing the table, I went to my room to finish my homework when I heard the door open again. Eric was back. He had flowers, I'm sure. Daisies, was my guess, since that was Mom's favorite. I quietly peeked my head around the door to see him standing at the door with his arms outstretched offering his version of, "I'm sorry." Mom continued with the dishes, refusing to look at him. "Good," I thought to myself before returning to my books.

Moments later, as he planted himself in front of the TV, with his chicken potpie, Mom returned to her paper. To avoid the thick tension, I gave Em a bath. Being unaware of what had transpired, she brought much-needed comic relief. As she popped each of the bubbles, I grinned. I pulled her hair into a mohawk, and before rinsing, I grabbed a mirror from under the sink and held it up for her to see. She clapped, splashing water with delight.

I pulled Em out of the bath, keeping her towel tightly wrapped so as not to drip on the floor. I knew that would be too much for Mom to handle. *The straw that broke the camel's back*, as she'd say. As Em squirmed free, I realized she had no clean pajamas. I unearthed the pile of laundry sitting atop of the hamper. The sour aroma caused my stomach to revolt and my eyes to water. I wondered when the last time Mom had done laundry was. She was so busy picking up the pieces of Eric's mistakes that she had forgotten daily chores. I re-entombed the stench, piling the laundry back on top of the hamper. I struggled to put a pull-up on Em's bare bottom and suggested we read a story.

Em scribbled with crayons while I read the Peanuts book "Happiness Is" to her. This was Mom's favorite book as a little girl. It had "Angie Hawthorne, Age 6, KLM 0065" written in the cover with a barrage of hearts and smiley faces adorning the page. I wondered what had happened to make her life veer so far from that carefree little girl of the past. I teared up as I read out loud "Happiness Is… a Warm Blanket." I reached over for Em's striped baby blanket and folded it warmly into her arms. She smiled and said, "Blankey!" before nuzzling into its soft fringe.

I cuddled her for just a moment and put her in bed. I buried my face in my pillow as the tears came, silently praying.

2

The morning sun streamed into the room as my alarm hollered, alerting me that six o'clock had arrived. As my eyes adjusted to the light, I squinted, wishing for just a few more minutes. I could hear Em playing in her crib, so I peeked my eyes open just a little bit. Her gaze landed on me and she giggled. I couldn't help but smile.

I rose from my bed and stretched my arms to the ceiling before dropping to my knees and placing my hands on the bars of the crib. Em squealed with delight as I made funny faces at her through the bars.

Not wanting to draw attention to myself, I crept out the door. I saw my Mom and Eric eating breakfast holding hands across the table. I tentatively stepped forward.

Mom jumped up, "Josie! Happy Birthday, baby!" She ran over to give me a hug and kiss. For a moment, I had forgotten it was my birthday.

Mom smiled and said, "Things are going to get better, Josie. I know we had a rough night last night, but Eric is really sorry. He loves us and wants us to be a family."

Eric's eyes pointed toward his plate of eggs. With his fork, he drew through the eggs, leaving trails of yolk behind.

"Ok," was all I could think of to say.

Mom continued, "Eric is going to be getting some side-work and things will start looking up soon."

Eric sat still, staring into his eggs. He wore a black jacket around his shoulders. Hunched over his plate, his black hair fell over his eyes and stubble adorned his jaw. I wondered why he didn't say anything if he was so sorry, but said nothing.

Something about the way he was dressed and the dishonesty over his face made me feel on edge.

"Don't you have something you'd like to say to Josie?"

"Happy Birthday, kid," he muttered as he grabbed his brown bag lunch and made his way out the door. His work boots were still lying on the floor as he stepped over them. Mom didn't notice.

"Sissy!" Em exclaimed as I poked my head around the door in peek-a-boo fashion. She gleefully giggled as we played this game. Finally, knowing I had limited time, I jumped in and yelled, "Surprise!" She jumped up and down in her crib, barely able to contain her excitement. I untangled her from the many blankets and snuggled my face in her neck. I set her down and she toddled in to greet Mom.

While Mom made eggs for us, I gathered up my homework, making sure it was all completed. I tossed it in my backpack and threw on my clothes.

I scarfed down the overly runny eggs and gave Mom a thumbs-up. The grumble and growl of the bus barreling down the street behind my house caused me to throw down my fork and jump up, knowing it would be in front within a minute; I hurriedly brushed my teeth and scrambled out the door. I made it to the curb just as the bus rounded the corner.

I hopped on and bumped through the elbows and backpacks to find a seat next to Jessie. Upon dropping my backpack next to me, a nudge prompted me to look up at her. She nodded her head toward an older guy at the front of the bus.

"He's the bus driver's son. He's kinda cute, huh?" She said without taking her eyes off him.

I quickly glanced at him, realizing he was older and replied with a slight smile. He was cute, but Jessie always went for older boys. The bus driver, Jeanie, had her eyes locked on him, as worry crept along her face.

"I wonder what he's doing on the bus," I said to Jessie.

"Shelly thinks he got kicked outta high school," she whispered, "but she doesn't know. She's all talk." Just then, Shelly interjected, "That's what my mom's friend said. That he was caught in the girl's bathroom and they kicked him out."

School isn't too far from my house. Our town is small, with everything you need in one spot, but go 5 miles in any direction, and you'll hit a highway, forest, or farmland.

At the last pickup, a classmate named Lacey hopped on the bus with headphones on, throwing out the hip-hop vibe. Her ponytail swung as she bounced down the aisle. The stranger on the bus eyed her as she moved.

Lacey liked attention and it was apparent she noticed the new face on the bus as well. She was the kind of girl all the boys like and all the girls want to be like with all the best clothes and newest trends. She doesn't talk to me much.

She's never been mean to me, but she is friends with the popular girls. I realized as I stared at her, that I was jealous of her home, her family, her clothes, and the hip-hop spraying out of her headphones.

I was ripped from my daydream when the bus screeched to a halt, horns blared, and backpacks launched to the floor. I looked out the window as a white truck rolled ahead, ignoring its near miss.

3

The day went by slowly. I had a lot on my mind, wondering and worrying about Eric. Uneasiness crept into my activities that day. I was nominated to be hall monitor recently, which is really more a job in which you help the teachers than it is of monitoring anything. I was so distracted by things at home that I nearly plowed into the janitor, only it wasn't our usual janitor.

"Uh, sorry," I said, too embarrassed to look at him for more than a second.

"It's okay, babe" he said in a deep voice. He smelled like cigarettes.

Babe? I thought to myself, *how weird.*

I continued without looking back. I delivered our lunch count to the office and returned to our classroom in time for math.

My mind was in a cloud for the rest of the day.

At lunch, I said to Jessie, "Mom and Eric were fighting again last night, but then today everything was weirdly perfect."

"Don't you hate when parents act like everything is fine? Like we're stupid or something," Jessie replied as she unwrapped her sandwich.

"No, it's not like they were trying to keep something from me. The weird thing is that I think they both believed it. Like they know nothing is good, but putting on a smile and saying things are getting better will make them better," I countered.

Just then, two boys came to our table and sat down. Jessie turned her attention to them. With a bat of her eyes and the flip of her hair, she was no longer interested in my problems.

I gathered my trash and said, "Well, I'll see you later. Gotta get to class."

***

I managed to keep the troubling thoughts to myself for the rest of the afternoon. After computer class, Mrs. Cambrio sent me to the office with schoolwork for a sick classmate. On my way there, I slipped and nearly fell before feeling a grip on my arm.

"Be more careful there," a voice said. I took my arm from his grip and overwhelmed with embarrassment, picked up the books from the floor and walked into the office. I looked back. This janitor was younger than the other one we referred to as Smiley. He stood, still looking at me with his squared-off jaw, dark complexion, and spikey hair. Twice now, I had been in a daze and knocked into this guy. What was wrong with me?

I had just two minutes before the final bell would ring, and hurried back toward the classroom, stopping by my locker on the way.

As the final bell clanged in my ears, I gathered my books before being abruptly knocked off kilter. It was Lacey.

"I'm sorry, Josie!" It was weird hearing her say my name. We had never really talked to each other, but I smiled back and answered her saying, "Wanna sit together on the bus?" Immediately regretting my response, I was sure she would look at me as if I were a weirdo.

"Sure," she said.

Really? I thought to myself.

I knew Jessie would be mad when she found out I had given up her seat next to me, but this was Lacey Stewart! I wanted to be one of the popular girls, or at least noticed by one of them.

Lacey and I walked together to the bus and found an open seat.

"What kind of music do you listen to?" she asked excitedly.

"Anything on Hot 97," I answered, figuring it was a safe bet. I didn't have a CD player of my own, though, much less an MP3 player, so I mostly listened to my mom's music, which consisted of Journey and REO Speedwagon.

Her eyes lit up as she stretched the headphones over to my ears so I could hear, too. It's brand new. My dad got it for me."

"Cool," I smiled. My head bobbing to Nickelback's, *Far Away*, I closed my eyes and let the music fill my thoughts. When the song ended, I opened my eyes to see her looking at me with eager eyes. I took the headphones off and asked, "What?"

She giggled and said, "I asked you if you could come over today."

"I can't. It's my birthday. I have plans with my family." Fearful she would change her mind about me, I added a quick, "How about tomorrow?"

Her smile returned as she exclaimed, "Hey, it's your golden birthday! November 13th. You were born in 1993, same as me, right? You turn 13?"

I answered with a smile and a nod.

The bus came to a stop and she jumped off with a bounce in her step. Turning back to find me looking out the window, she gave a signal with her pinkie pointing toward her mouth and her thumb toward her ear, as if to say, *Call me*. As I waved out the window, I caught a glimpse of a grey Blazer as it nearly backed into another car in the parking lot of Kramer's Pharmacy. It looked like Eric's truck, but it couldn't be him because he wouldn't be off work yet.

"That would have really broken that camel's back," I uttered under my breath.

Jessie took the spot where Lacey had been sitting. With her mouth drawn down, her eyes wordlessly asking why I hadn't sat with her.

I shrugged and told her, "I'm here now," with a smile. Jessie asked questions about Lacey during the rest of the bus ride. She was as interested in *the life of Lacey Stewart* as I was, though I could tell she was jealous that Lacey asked me over instead of her. Before arriving at my stop, Jessie wished me a happy birthday before getting off the bus. This made me feel even worse about not sitting with her. Having Lacey interested in talking to me, befriending me, was too tempting.

A few hours later, I was setting the table when I heard the key in the door. Mom welcomed Eric home with a kiss as he came through the door. He looked better than he had this morning.

He was clean-shaven now; his hair combed back, though still too long, falling past his collar.

He was smiling and said, "Birthday tacos— was that your choice, kid?" I smiled and nodded.

"How about kid's choice out instead?" Although this changed seemed odd, I looked at my mom who was beaming. I smiled and got my coat while Mom scooped up the taco meat to save for later.

"Grab the van keys, Angie. A guy from work is borrowing the Blazer tonight," Eric said, as he pulled his coat on and shuffled out the door. Em was toddling toward me, shoes in hand, asking to go bye-bye, too. I slapped on her shoes and threw a coat on her before zipping it up and closing the button tightly against her chin. I noticed Mom was wearing lipstick and mascara when she emerged from her bedroom ready to leave. I hadn't seen Mom out of her over-sized shirt, pajama pants, and her hair pulled tightly in a ponytail for a long time. I actually believed there may be a change on the horizon.

We jumped in the van and after buckling Em in her pumpkin seat, we were on our way to Pizza King.

Over pizza, Eric told Mom that things were going to be different.

"Angie, we aren't going to have to worry anymore. Things will get better. I'm back on at work, and there's tons of overtime."

Mom looked in my direction. With tears in my eyes, I gave a slight smile.

When we arrived at home, there were three packages wrapped in the weekend funnies on the coffee table. I was shocked to open two books and a sweater, believing I wouldn't get anything this year. I knew Mom and Eric were struggling, so when our electricity was shut off last month, I prepared myself for a gift-less birthday.

"Wow, Mom, I didn't expect this at all!" I ran to try the sweater on. It fit and was so comfy! I slid my hands up and down my arms feeling the plush turquoise yarn as it fluffed against my fingers.

"Josie, you look beautiful!" Mom said, "Do you like it? How does it fit?"

"I love it Mom, it's perfect!" I exclaimed as I turned, modeling the sweater.

I blew out my birthday candles and remembered my plans for the following day.

"Hey Mom, can I go to a friend's house after school tomorrow?"

"I don't see why not, Jo." Mom shorted my name to Jo from Josie or Josephine when she was in her best moods. "Who is it? Do I know her? Will her parents be home?" She questioned in triplicate.

"I'm sure they will be, Mom," I answered, adding, "It's a girl named Lacey in my class. She lives a few miles away by car, but it's not really that far if you cut through the neighborhoods. She even rides my bus."

"Is she in the Buzz Book? I'll call her mom to confirm," she added.

"Ok, I'm sure she's in there – last name Stewart," I said, while pulling out the Buzz Book. I opened it to "S" and handed it to my mom.

I took my plate to the sink and skipped to my room to plan my outfit for the next day. I picked out my best jeans, setting my new turquoise sweater on top.

I looked over the clothes as they lay across my floor, beaming.

"Josie…." Mom called from the living room.

"Yeah," I answered, as I turned the corner approaching the hallway.

Mom was sitting on the couch writing on a sheet of paper. "I was able to reach Lacey's parents. They said you were welcome to come over after school. I wrote a note to let the office and bus driver know you'll be getting off at Lacey's stop tomorrow afternoon," she said while handing me the folded slip of paper.

I reached down to retrieve the note, slipping it into my backpack slumped against the nearby wall. As I started back toward my room, I heard her say, "Wait, one more thing." I turned on my heels and looked at her, my face inquisitively awaiting her reply.

She smiled as she placed her hands on her lap, poised to rise. Looking up me, she stood and said, "There's something out here, too," as she walked toward the garage.

I slowly walked toward the garage door. "What is it?" I inquired with a hand on the doorknob. I turned the knob, curious as to what I would find. Sitting in the garage was a blue 10-speed bike. I ran my fingers over the blue paint, stunned by the turn of events. I had hoped for a new bike for the last two Christmases. I mounted the seat, placing my right foot on the pedal and resting my palms on the handlebars.

"Smile!" prompted Mom, as I sat, stunned, on my new 10-speed. I looked up and smiled, allowing the grin to spread across my face, capturing the excitement of the moment forever as she clicked away on the camera.

"It's from Eric," Mom said. He got a bonus and decided it was time to get you a new bike!"

"Thanks!" I exclaimed. He barely looked at me, but said, "Sure thing, kid," with a smile creeping on his face.

"Can I ride it for a few minutes?" I begged.

"I don't know... It's pretty dark," Mom answered.

Noting my anticipation, she looked up in thought. Chewing on the inside of her cheek, she paused a moment before relenting saying, "Just a few minutes."

I nudged the kickstand up and sped out of the garage toward the road. As I descended the hill, I felt the sensation of butterfly wings kissing my cheeks. Even in the cold air, I felt warm. I felt free as the wind carried with it my flowing hair. I heard Mom yell, "Don't go far!" as I pedaled my way past the nearest cross street.

4

Eager to begin my day, I was up before my alarm. I admired myself in the mirror wearing my new sweater before laying a strip of paste over the bristles of my toothbrush.

"Josie, I'll drop your bike at Lacey's house this afternoon so you can ride it after school," Mom said as she passed by the bathroom. With a mouthful of toothpaste, I acknowledged her comment, saying, "mm hm" through my teeth.

I quickly gathered my things and yelled bye to Mom, shutting the front door behind me. The air was warmer, no need for a coat, just my new sweater would do.

Hearing the bus' loud rumble, I struggled to pull on my backpack, wondering why the bus was early. I sat back down as I realized it was just another loud, grumbling truck. It slowed a bit, as if the driver was lost. It was a tall truck with an upward sliding door in back. The side of the truck displayed faded blue letters over a dingy white surface. All I could make out was S....ke..t...D..iv.ry. As I secretly wished I were the one getting something delivered, the truck took off. Guilt crept into my stomach as I silently scolded myself for thinking that way after getting such great gifts yesterday. Year after year, however, I silently wished that I would wake up on my birthday to a package from Dad. Although my birthday had passed, I still hoped he remembered me. I was starting to forget him. It had been so long since I had seen him. He just up and disappeared one day – never to be heard from again. He never really spent much time with me, or even read me a book or tucked me in. I felt like he left because he didn't want me. Year after year, I always hoped he'd come back with some great reason as to why he had been gone and how much he missed me.

Moments later, the sound of the gargling bus disrupted my thoughts. I hopped on looking for Jessie. She was seated, waiting for me. I was happy she didn't seem mad. She immediately asked what I got for my birthday. She was thrilled I got a new bike so we could ride together now. I could no longer ride my old bike–not only was it too small, but the tires had deteriorated from age and wear. At Lacey's stop, Jessie looked at me as if to ask if she was still welcome to sit with me.

I nodded and said, "Sure, we can all sit together."

Lacey's ponytail bobbed as she strode toward our seats. She sat across from us, sticking her feet out so we could admire her new pair of shoes as we oohed and ahhed.

"Are you still coming over after school?" she asked.

"Yeah, I can come," I answered.

"Cool!" she exclaimed with a smile. "Jessie, you should come, too!" she suggested. Jessie's eyes lit up. "I'll call my mom from the office and see if it's okay!" she said a little too eagerly.

I smiled to myself knowing that's how I sounded yesterday.

After school, the three of us hopped the bus and sat together until we reached Lacey's stop. As we walked from the bus stop, I beamed hearing Lacey talk about how much she wanted to be friends with us. Turning the corner and making our way down the sidewalk of her court, we saw her beautiful home with large windows adorning the front and its expansive front door with glass inserts gracing the entry beyond a sprawling porch. From the driveway, I could see a large back yard and in-ground pool. Wishing it were summer, I said, "You are so lucky you have your own pool!"

"Yeah, we'll have some great pool parties this summer," she said eagerly. "You should come!"

"Definitely," I said while nodding.

The abounding foyer greeted us as we entered her home. It was as clean as a museum. I wondered what she would think of my house – where there was just one bathroom for us all to share, and where Em and I shared a room.

Lacey's room was blanketed in pink. She had a beautiful four-poster bed covered in a pink canopy. In the corner of her room was a pink and white recliner next to a table holding her very own phone.

We spent the afternoon playing games, talking about boys, and riding bikes around her neighborhood.

Lacey led us to a creek nearby where we sat on the bank and rested while picking at the dead grass.

"How come we've never talked much before?" I asked, looking at Lacey.

"'Cause you two always sat together and we kinda have our own group of friends. I always liked you and thought you were both nice, though."

"I didn't think you liked us," I said quietly with a slight chuckle.

"What reason would I have to not like you?"

"We're so different. You have a mom *and* a dad; you live in a really great neighborhood in a huge house. I have a tiny house, hand-me-downs, and a crazy step-dad."

"I don't care about that stuff. Things aren't always what they seem on the outside, believe me," she said matter-of-factly.

Jessie piped up to add, "Yeah, but you've never really talked to us, and we've been at the same school and riding the same bus for years. I'm glad you invited us. We should make this a regular thing. We don't live far at all. I think the park is half-way between all our houses."

I stood, indicating I was ready to go, smiling at my newfound friendship.

On our way back to Lacey's house, we passed a courier truck. The driver peered oddly at us from underneath his low-set baseball cap as he crept through the stop sign.

"That's the second time I've seen that truck today. Plus another truck before it," I recalled aloud.

"It's almost Christmas," Jessie noted. "These trucks are all over the place helping deliver packages."

An hour later, we were at Lacey's house, finishing dinner and starting on homework when my mom came to the door to pick me up.

***

For the next two weeks, the three of us were inseparable. We found a shortcut between our houses and began meeting halfway to walk with one another through the park separating our neighborhoods. On the Tuesday before Thanksgiving, while riding the bus home from school, the three of us decided to celebrate the following day off school by going to the movies.

"What movie are you going to see?" a voice inquired from the next seat over. It was the bus driver's son, Frankie. He continued to be on the bus day after day over the last two weeks.

"The Holiday," Jessie said, without missing a beat.

"So, what did you do to get kicked outta school?" Lacey asked him without hesitation.

"Lacey!" I exclaimed.

"Frankie didn't get kicked out of high school," Jessie answered, "he was suspended for two weeks."

Looking at her with furrowed brows, I wondered how Jessie found out his story. "How'd you find that out?"

She smiled with a sly grin without answering.

"What for?" Lacey inquired.

"Somethin' I didn't do," he answered, adding, "My ex-girlfriend, Anna, she saw me coming out of the girls' bathroom. Someone plugged the sinks and flooded the bathroom, so I got busted for it."

I looked at him suspiciously. "I swear!" he said, hands up and eyes wide, adding "It wasn't me! They didn't have any proof, that's why I only got two weeks suspension instead of being expelled," he continued with a smile on his face. "The only reason they busted me was 'cause I wasn't in class at the time."

Jessie looked up at him with stars in her eyes, wholeheartedly believing every word.

Mom dropped us off at the arcade about an hour before the movie was to start. Lacey, Jessie, and I were playing skee-ball when Jessie felt a tap on her shoulder. Frankie smiled when she turned around.

Her eyes lit up as she asked, "Hey, what are you doing here?"

"I came to see you," he said in a cool voice. "And some of my buddies are here, too," he added as he shoved his car keys in his pocket.

Frankie introduced Josh and Max to us. When he was finished, Josh looked behind him and waved another boy forward. "That's Mason. He's 14. We met playing Mortal Kombat. His uncle's over there," he said, pointing to a dark corner. "He's watching our every move," he warned with an eye roll.

I squinted, bringing the corner in to focus and saw a man holding a cigarette, eyeing us intently.

Frankie and Jessie interlocked hands and went to the back of the arcade. She stood with her back to the wall, looking up into Frankie's eyes.

Lacey and I stood awkwardly with Max, Josh, and Mason near the ticket counter.

I broke the silence asking, "Where do you go to school?"

"Max and I go to Jefferson High with Frankie," Josh answered.

"We're on the football team. You should come to a game sometime," Max interrupted, looking at me.

I smiled. "And what about you, where do you go?" I asked, looking at Mason.

Josh answered for him, "He said he's homeschooled," then turned his attention toward Lacey, leaving me between Mason and Max. Mason said nothing, but he kept looking at me under his long hair. Each time our eyes met he quickly looked away. He was dressed in dark clothes, his dark unkempt hair long and hanging over his face.

Max interrupted my thoughts. "Your name's Josie, right? Frankie told me a lot about you," Max said while leaning on the counter, looking up at me. His dark complexion suggested a Latino background. He was handsome, and he knew it. He took his jacket off, showing muscles beneath his tight-fitting shirt.

"Mhmm," I said, as he continued looking deep into my eyes. I looked away from his dimpled smile, nervous under his gaze.

I excused myself and pulled Lacey aside. "I don't think we should be here. I don't want to get in trouble," I admitted.

"Your parents don't expect you to stay home and never have fun, Josie. It's not like we knew they would be here," Lacey said as she led me back to the group.

I had always been "the responsible one." Not to mention my shyness around boys. Feeling like I misled my mom about what we were doing today, guilt attacked my soul.

Twenty minutes later, Jessie walked over and pulled me aside saying, "Josie, Max is soooo into you! He's cute, don't you think?"

"Yeah, he's cute, but he's like 17, isn't he?" I asked.

"No, he's 15, and it's not like you have to marry the guy! Jeez!"

"Still, I've never even had a boyfriend," I countered.

"I'm really nervous. I don't know what to do or say. I don't know what to do with my hands. He looks deep into my eyes, almost as if he's trying to see through me. He's just too intense." I smiled, hoping she would understand. "Oh, and Mason is the opposite. He doesn't talk at all, yet I could feel his stare boring into my skin while Max was talking to me. I just really want to go. Let's go to the movies, now, okay?" I suggested, hoping she would take me up on my offer.

Jessie rolled her eyes, but agreed. "You are way too shy. You'll never get a boyfriend if you don't talk to boys!" She sounded serious, but offered a smile as she hooked her arm into mine and led us to the boys. We said goodbye and Jessie and Frankie exchanged numbers. The boys left, and I gave a quick wave to Mason before watching him make his way slowly back to his uncle.

***

The Thursday following Thanksgiving, an ice storm cut the power to our house. Mom, Em, and I lit candles and to fill the silence, Mom began inquiring about my new friendship with Lacey as she began dealing out the cards for Gin Rummy.

"You and Lacey are spending a lot of time together lately. And you seem really happy, Jo," she said.

"I really like her, Mom. She's nice, and funny, and she makes me try new things. I feel freer when I'm with her," I added, smiling.

"I thought it would be nice if you invite her over here so we can get to know her better, too. Would you like to have her for a sleepover tomorrow?" Mom asked.

"YES!" I couldn't contain my excitement! I hadn't had someone for a sleepover. I hadn't seen much of Eric lately; things almost seemed like the old days, and I wondered if that's why I was allowed to have a sleepover.

I dialed Lacey's number and when she answered, I squealed, "Can you spend the night tomorrow?!" She squealed back and asked her mom, returning shortly to the phone and told me, "She said yes!"

"Ok, my mom says four o'clock," Iconfirmed, adding, "Do you want to meet up or have your mom drop you off?"

"I can walk – maybe we can meet half-way," she suggested.

"Sure, that way I can help you carry your stuff the rest of the way."

"Yeah, that sounds good, four o'clock at the park," Lacey confirmed.

The next morning, Mom and I moved Em's crib into her room and set up the bunk bed for Lacey and me. I was counting down the minutes until 4pm when I would meet Lacey at the park.

5

I left the house early, giving myself plenty of time to arrive by four o'clock. It was colder than I thought it would be. I regretted our decision to meet, wishing we had arranged to have Lacey's mom drop her off at my house.

I stepped recklessly onto the back porch, catching myself on the rail as my foot slipped beneath me. Drawing a breath in, I remembered the ice storm the night before. Taking a more precise step forward, my now steady boots landed in the crisp snow, a loud crunch sounding beneath my feet. I pulled the boots from their mold and took a large step forward to avoid kicking the blanket of ice-capped snow.

I walked to the farthest point of our yard and followed the tree line to where I would soon meet the crosswalk just feet away from the wooded path. My breath misted into white puffy clouds before blending into the cold, grey backdrop. I heard a rumble in the distance and looked up to see a white truck slowly drive past as I gained ground, making my way closer to the crosswalk.

I continued my trek through the shimmering ice-packed snow, my teeth chattering involuntarily. The wind rendezvoused with the snowflakes as they drifted down from a cold, unforgiving sky. I shrugged my shoulders against my neck, inviting it into the combined warmth of my coat and fur-lined hood.

I plunged a naked fist into my pockets in search of gloves. Approaching the sidewalk, I slid one glove over my glaciated fingers, unintentionally dropping the other on the curb. While I bent to retrieve it, I heard the gargling engine as it rolled closer.

I studied the truck. It looked like the delivery truck with the overhead door I had seen before. It came to a stop just past the crosswalk. The glove slipped my mind as I wondered why the truck had stopped.

A man wearing dark clothes, a hat, and sunglasses, dismounted from the truck, with a clipboard in hand calling, "You live over there, yeah?" pointing behind him.

"Uh-huh," I answered over the shrill cry of the overhead door as he slid it up and jumped in the opening.

"Your name – It's uh…" he started, as I heard boxes being moved around.

"Josie," I answered.

"Yeah, yeah. Josie. That's right. I got boxes in here with your name on 'em," he called.

"What? –Oh, ok," I said. I hadn't had a package delivered for me before. *Packages with my name on them?* I wondered. I asked myself, *did Dad remember my birthday this year? Christmas was just about one month away – did Mom order something? She said things would be getting better.* Disorganized excitement spun through my mind, while I contemplated the possibilities.

"Well, you comin' or aren't ya? These ain't gonna deliver themselves," a muffled voice from inside yelled.

I smiled as I hoisted myself into the back of the truck ready for my package to be placed into my hands. "It's that one, back there in the corner, the white box," he directed.

I beamed as I walked closer to the front, near the truck's cabin, daydreaming about the package contents.

As I reached to grab the package, the driver jumped out to the street causing the truck to shift. I lost my footing, planting my hand on the side of the truck for support. I lifted the feather-light box, realizing slowly that it didn't have my name on it. *Wait*, I thought. *No name. No address – it was blank.*

I lightly nudged the other boxes, and in doing so sent them flying, unearthing the truth. This wasn't a delivery truck. I turned toward the open door and saw him. Like a tiger watching its prey, his eyes slyly drawn into slits; a smirk adorning his face. With my mouth agape, my eyes pleaded with him. He raised an eyebrow and mouthed, "Gotchya," as he jerked the overhead door's handle. I stood paralyzed, listening to the shrieking outcry of the door as he heaved it shut.

6

At 5 minutes till 4:00, she shouted, "I'm going to meet Josie now!"

Her mom ran down the stairs. "Lacey, are you sure you don't want me to drive you?" she asked.

"No. It's fine," she answered, as she gave her a quick hug and kiss.

Grabbing her heavy coat on the way out, she set her duffle bag down to pull the coat on, buttoning it up to the top before placing the duffle bag crosswise over her body. She tucked her pillow under her arm and started on her way.

Five minutes later, she was waiting for Josie at their usual meeting spot. Feeling the temperature plummet, she cinched up her coat and pulling a knit cap from her pocket, she pulled it over her ears and readjusted the coat's hood, allowing it to double up the warmth. Her teeth chattered as her body convulsed from the prickling cold.

She began to move, aerobics-like, in an attempt to warm up her body. Five minutes later, she looked at her watch, wondering how much longer she'd have to wait. Replaying their conversation in her head, she thought, *did she say I should just come all the way to her house?*

No. She was going to meet me halfway to make sure I could make it with my stuff.

She continued to wait as the sun started to descend into the trees.

The chilling, wet snow seeped into her boots, leaving her toes cold and stiff, she contemplated whether she should go back to her house or walk the rest of the way to Josie's. *My house it is. At least I could get some new socks. Mine had become soaked, after all,* she considered.

She shot in through the door and went right for the vents, ripping off her boots and soaked socks in one swift motion. She felt the thaw, and a yelp of pain erupted from her lips.

Her mom ran into the room in angst.

"Oh, it's you! What are you doing home?" she asked, with her hand over her chest.

"Josie never showed up," Lacey answered.

With a puzzled look she said, "That's weird."

"And it's not like her at all," she added.

After walking out of the room, Lacey's mom behind her, "be back in a sec!" A moment later, she called from the kitchen, "How long did you wait, Lacey?"

"Like 15 minutes. At least."

A few moments later, she heard her mom's heels click against the linoleum. Looking up, she sighed as she spotted the warm mug of hot chocolate. Wrapping her cold hands around the mug, she allowed the warmth to enter her fingertips.

Lacey's mom kicked off her heels and sat next to her daughter on the floor. Wrapping her arms around Lacey's trembling body, she slid her hands up and down Lacey's arms to generate heat. After handing her the phone, she said, "You'd better call. Maybe she was running late. Tell her mom I'll drive you. It's too dark to walk now."

Lacey couldn't help but wonder if she had the plans wrong. The sick feeling she'd been suppressing sunk deeper into her stomach as she slowly dialed the phone number.

7

"Hello?" Mrs. McIntosh answered.

"Yes, Mrs. McIntosh, um, this is Lacey."

"Oh, hello, Lacey! Where are you girls? Did you forget something?" she asked.

"No, ma'am," she said. "I waited for Josie, but she never showed."

There was silence on the other end.

"Mrs. McIntosh?" Waiting for an answer, she looked to her mom for direction.

"Lacey, you met Josie at the park, right?" she recalled.

"I went to the park, but she wasn't there. I thought maybe I got the time wrong or something and came back home."

Mrs. McIntosh yelled for Eric as Lacey's mom tugged the phone from her hands.

"Angie," she interrupted. "Angie, it's Kathy... What's going on?"

She could only hear one side on the conversation now as her mom stood up and started walking away. She spoke calmly into the phone, "Yes, 20 minutes ago at least... Yes, she said she waited for over 15 minutes for her. I'm sure... We'll be right there."

Moments later, they were at Josie's house. Questions spewed from all directions. Lacey's stomach hurt. Her lips were trembling and her legs felt like jelly. She could barely stand. Lacey covered her face with her hands and started rocking back and forth on her knees, trying to stifle the ringing in her ears. *Maybe she fell down. Was she freezing in the snow?* she wondered.

Lacey's dad arrived shortly after her mom called him. He and Eric agreed to walk the path Josie would have taken. They walked out the back door, blankets in hand, both gripping flashlights.

Eric turned and said to Angie through the door, "We'll find her. Don't do anything until we get back."

With her arms outstretched before her, she brought one up to her lips. "The police," she said with her eyes wide. "We should call the police."

"Not yet, Ang," he said. "They'll say it hasn't been enough time anyway. Wait–just until we get back." With that, they turned and began retracing Josie's steps.

Mrs. McIntosh grabbed her keys from the counter and ran out the garage door stammering, "I—I can't stay here doing nothing."

"Don't worry," Lacey's mom said with her hand on Angie's. "We'll stay here in case she calls or comes home. Lacey can help me watch Em, too."

Lacey opened the door just a crack. While the garage door muted her voice, she could still see Angie's face from the car. Her thumbs drummed nervously on the steering wheel; lifting them every few moments she wringed her fingers in distress. Her eyes were heavy with tears pouring down her cheeks. She put her head down on the steering wheel.

When the garage door had finished squealing, Lacey put her ear to the opening and heard her mom say, "Angie, you aren't fit to drive. Wait for the guys to get back and I can go with you."

"I can't leave my baby out there, Kathy," she answered, sobbing. "What if she's cold? Or scared?" she added.

Seconds later, Lacey's mom backed up from the car window and watched Angie back out of the driveway. She yelled to her, "We'll find her, Angie. If she's not back by the time you get home, we'll call the police."

Ten minutes had passed. Em was playing with blocks, and although Lacey was supposed to be playing with her, she couldn't stop worrying about Josie. Biting her upper lip, trying to convince herself that Angie would return with Josie any minute, she prayed.

There was a knock at the door. Lacey and her mom looked at each other before dashing to answer it.

Lacey held her breath as she turned the knob. She opened to see Jessie and her mom. Shawna, Jessie's mom, walked in exclaiming, "I just heard! What can we do?" with Jessie trailing behind.

"She never showed," Lacey said to Jessie. "I was supposed to spend the night, and she never showed to meet me."

"They'll find her," Jessie assured Lacey.

Shortly after, Lacey's dad came back with Eric. She could tell Josie was not with them, as she saw sorrow in her dad's eyes.

"She was nowhere to be found, Lacey. There aren't even tracks in the snow back there. Are you sure she was going to meet you?" he asked.

She nodded and managed only to ask, "then where is she, Dad?"

He reached a comforting warm hand over her head before guiding her gently to his chest. She held her breath, willing herself not to cry.

He stroked her hair and in a shaky voice said, "It's going to be alright." At that, he quickly backed up as they heard the garage door rise.

Lacey looked up at him. "The garage," he said, with his eyes wide. They ran to the garage door and watched as Josie's mom exited the van and shook her head, covering her face with her hands. Eric took Josie's mom by the arm and eased her into the house; looking fearful she would break.

8

(Four Hours Missing)

"Ma'am, please calm down. I realize this is difficult, but you need to stay as calm as possible. It's imperative you are able to give us as much detail about your daughter as possible," the Detective said.

He took a seat beside Josie's mom and said, "My name is Detective Falcor. I know this is an unimaginable situation, but I am here to help. The more information we can gather about your daughter, the arrangements she had today, the people she hangs out with, and the family and friends she comes into contact with, the better."

"She's 13 with brown hair and hazel eyes," she answered.

Detective Falcor nodded and said, "That's good, that's exactly the kind of information we need," as he wrote the information in his notebook.

"Mrs. McIntosh… Angie, right? Can I call you Angie?"

She nodded.

"I have additional questions for you, and my partner, Detective Silba will be talking to your husband. Is there somewhere she can take him to have their interview?" He asked as her face turned sickly. "Don't worry. It's standard procedure to rule out family members in order to move forward with the investigation," he added.

"I see," she said and directed Detective Silba with a head tilt toward the left before answering, "Yes, they are welcome to use the den."

As Detective Silba took Eric into the den, Detective Falcor continued with Josie's mom.

"Now, what is Josie's height and weight?" he asked.

"A—about, um… I'm not sure. She hasn't had her physical yet this year. She wears a 14 in girls," she answered.

Lacey piped up, "She's the same size as me. Same shoe size and everything – a 7 ½."

Detective Falcor gave her a smile and said, "So about …"

She wrinkled her face, trying to think, "About 4 feet, 10 inches tall and 90 pounds?" she answered, not completely sure.

"Great," he said as he wrote. "Now, where were the girls supposed to meet?" he asked. Angie looked over and said, "Barney Park, right, Lacey? Josie said there is a well-formed path through the woods. Not even a 5-minute walk."

Lacey looked up. "Yeah, we always meet at the same spot. We've been meeting at the park just on the other side of the woods. It's about halfway between her house and mine. Like Mrs. McIntosh said, it's like 5 minutes."

"Okay, and would there be any reason for her to have decided not meet you, Lacey?" he asked.

"No, not at all," she answered. "We talked about our plans for tonight. Either my mom would bring me over or we'd meet halfway. I know she wouldn't have left me because I had to carry all of my stuff."

"Because you were spending the night here," he finished. "Would she have gone somewhere else? Has she met anyone or talked to anyone new lately?" he asked.

"No, she's not like that. She and I have gotten really close. She would have told me something like that!" she said angrily, her throat tightening as she choked back tears.

Detective Silba, having finished with Eric, interrupted just then. "Sweetie, we just have to check all avenues. We don't think she did anything wrong. She's not in trouble. We just want to find her."

Lacey stood with tears spilling over her lids, exclaiming, "I swear! She wouldn't have gone anywhere else. She was excited to have me over." With that, she crumbled to the couch in disbelief, wondering how this could be happening.

"Okay, that's good information. Thank you, Lacey," Detective Falcor said, ending the conversation.

"Angie, did you and Josie fight recently? Is there any reason she would have decided to run away?"

Angie looked straight at him and said, "No, my daughter is a good kid. She is a good student; she doesn't get in trouble at school.

She'd have no reason to run away." She held her eyes to his, affirmed in her conviction that Josie would never run away.

He paused for a moment, eyeing Josie's mom. Seemingly satisfied with her answer, he sighed. "Okay, what I need now," Detective Falcor said, "is a photo of Josie, along with a description of any moles, scars, or distinguishing features. Does she have her ears pierced? Braces? And what was she wearing when she left the house?"

She stood and walked to where picture frames were affixed to the wall. "She has her ears pierced, but doesn't have braces. She was wearing jeans. And a purple coat – a puffy one – with a fur-lined hood. I don't remember what shirt she was wearing, a sweatshirt – a pink one maybe," she said, unsure of herself.

As she frantically collected photos from their affixed frames, laying each one on the table she held her arm over her stomach, as if to stop herself from vomiting.

"This one is the most recent," she replied with her finger tapping on the image. Her eyes locked on Josie's smiling face while the tears, about to breech the edge of her lids, threatened to spill with the blink of her eye. "She has a small, light birthmark beneath her right eye. When she was little, I told her an angel kissed her there." The dam broke and tears spilled freely as she sobbed into her palms.

9

"Please!" I pleaded, sobbing hysterically. "Let me out! What do you want from me? What did I do?!"

I could hear the echo of my anguished voice as we rounded a corner sharply. *One left turn*, I thought as my head hit the right side of the truck. *That was probably Jennings Street we just turned on. Where is he taking me?* The tears blurred my vision. It was dark, so I couldn't see much anyway. There were cracks in the door of the truck, allowing little light to stream in.

I began stomping my boots into those crevices, hoping against hope that I could widen the gaps enough to stick my fingers through. If I did, would someone even notice?

The steel was strong – too strong. I decided I'd have to make enough noise or commotion for someone to notice. Maybe if we stopped, I could scream, could bang on the side and cause the truck to rock—something to arise suspicion in neighboring cars.

Suddenly the truck slowed to a stop. I banged, kicked, and screamed, just as I had planned, for what seemed like several minutes. We began to move again, this time, veering the other direction. *Ok, so that was a right, probably the light on Beemer Street,* I subconsciously thought to myself.

I was exhausted from just those few minutes of using every ounce of energy I had in an attempt to free myself from this prison. I decided to sit and pay attention to the directions, resting up for the next stop when I would, again, gather up the will to fight my way out of that dark, confining box.

We stayed in a straight line for several minutes before stopping and continuing forward again. *No turns there. I guess we're still on Beemer. It's a long road – goes out to the highway, I think.*

As small as our town is, it was hard to get a grasp on where we were. Moments later, we came to another stop. I repeated my earlier plan, screaming, "Please! Let me out!! Heellllllp!" I stepped back and ran toward the door using my shoulder in an attempt to bust through, hearing a pop as I did so. "Ahhhhhhhhhhh," I screamed, as I pulled my right upper arm to my body with my left hand. "Please … somebody!" I implored, as I beat my fists repeatedly on the door, howling as my shoulder ached in rebellion.

The truck lurched forward again. I pressed my back against the wall of the truck, allowing my body to slide downward. I laid my legs out before me and hung my head, shocked by the events. *Maybe this was the last light before the highway,* I thought. *Had we hit all green lights until this one*? I pulled strength from deep within myself to focus. *Most 13 year olds wouldn't have the town streets memorized*, I thought, but with the level of responsibility I had taken in the last several years since Dad left and mom married Eric, I knew I had it in me. *I had no choice,* I thought. *I have to fight.* I pulled the strength God gave me from deep within my gut to make it my mission to return to Mom and Em.

By now, I could tell by the sound that we were going over the river. Sometime later, the truck veered and made several turns before lurching to a stop. I heard the engine cut and cowered in the corner of the truck.

"What do you want?" I pleaded. For several minutes, I heard nothing. I decided to stand up and see if the cabin door would budge. I pulled and felt possibility. I yanked and the door gave, opening to the side. Realizing I was alone, I stepped through the opening. As I adjusted to the blazing white snow reflecting back at my stunned eyes, I saw a vast open space blanketed in snow. Beyond the clearing were snow-covered pine trees.

I can make it, I thought, yet wondering why he unlocked the door to begin with. Fearful that he would be waiting for me, ready to pounce, I convinced myself this was my only chance. *RUN!! NOW! GO!* I yelled at myself, willing my legs to move forward. The stabbing pain in my shoulder now an afterthought, I jumped out and saw my abductor peeing on the side of the truck.

"What the fuck do you think you're doing?" he yelled. I ran without answering, but even with cross-country training, I was no match for his stride.

He ran for me and yanked me by my ponytail. I crashed to the ground with a hard thud, hitting my shoulder and hearing a new 'pop!' I struggled to my feet, ready to run, when the back of his hand connected with my lip. I spit blood into his face as he wrapped his strong hand around my neck, forcing the last breath I held in my lungs to depart from my lips. As darkness faded in, I reached out, fingernails extended. *Thank you, God*, I thought, as I connected with his face, leaving two long, bloody crevices. I gave one good kick in the groin before he released his grip, simultaneously bringing one hand to his face and one hand to his groin while doubling over.

I ran with everything I had. I ran for my mom and Em. I ran for me.

10

I didn't dare look back. I reached the halfway point between the truck and the pine trees when I heard it. A low, but loud 'bang,' followed by echoing pops rang in the air.

The gravity of the situation hit me like the bullet that struck my leg.

"Nooo! No. This isn't happening!" I demanded my body to forge ahead, running, barely slowing until I reached the trees. My leg hurt, but not like I thought a gunshot would. I decided it must have grazed me and kept on.

In the trees, I moved forward, crouching low to the ground, hoping he wasn't following. Up until now, I had convinced myself not to look back. But now, I couldn't help myself. I glanced behind me, only to see the truck barreling toward the trees.

I hurried deeper into the woods, slowed by the bleeding of my leg. I had no time to nurse it.

It was getting dark in the dense trees. The sun would be down soon. I panned the trees looking for cover as I continued walking for at least an hour. I only stopped on occasion to pick up a handful of icy snow to drink.

Every noise was a potential threat. I walked when my body demanded, picking up the pace as best as I could.

The sun was going down fast now. In minutes, it would be completely gone. I looked up, already able to see the light shape of the moon in the sky.

I heaved my body up the hill, gripping trees propelling my body upward. When I crested the climb, I leaned against a thick oak tree, closing my eyes and catching my breath. Deciding it was time to move forward, I opened them and took a step toward my descent. About half-way down the climb, I noticed a structure to the left. I changed directions, now walking level with the steep hill, wincing, my thigh aching with every step.

I approached the structure from behind with caution. Eric hunted, occasionally sleeping in the woods, so I guessed that this structure was a lean-to offering a hunter shelter from the elements while they waited for their kill. I examined my surroundings, listening for signs of activity before making my entrance. There were cans and bottles in the corners of the lean-to, but it did not look inhabited.

I was thrilled to be out of the wind, deciding it was a good time to rest and nurse my leg. As I sat there, breathing deeply, family memories engulfed my mind in an attempt to free it from my current reality.

I sat for a moment, applying ice to my leg, realizing I hadn't cried in hours.

The emotional pain was excruciating.

I was missing… I was lost…I was being hunted. My reality caught up with me. I wanted my mom. I allowed myself a moment to let the tears come. It was a moment to grieve for my mom and Em, and to grieve for me and my childhood, and the possibility that I may not survive the night.

***

As I opened my eyes, the realization that this was not a horrific nightmare hit.

It was dark. I must have fallen asleep. My fingers and toes were stiff as I clenched my body tight, urging my body temperature to rise. I looked at my leg, which was heavily bleeding now. I wondered how much time had gone by. I looked around, not recognizing my surroundings. I suddenly wondered how long I might have been running before I stopped.

There was no time to lose. The air was getting colder. The longer I sat here, the narrower the gap would become between us.

I got up and decided to change directions, considering the options. Hoping I might be able to reach a main road. I walked for what seemed like hours. It was nearly pitch black now. I wasn't sure if I was even making any progress. I sucked on another chunk of ice. Nearby, I found a large stick to help take weight off my bad leg.

I walked on, looking for any sign of life, lights, cars—anything. Luckily, my shoulder was feeling good. I determined that it must have popped back into place when he threw me to the ground.

I had a lot of time to think during this time. I wondered what the best way out of something like this was. *If I get to a road, would I scream, run, and wave at someone to stop for me? Would they?* I wondered. *What if he finds me? Would I have it in me to fight him again? How will I survive? If he did capture me,* I thought to myself, *would he kill me?* The words echoed in my mind, "*Would he kill me...kill me... kill me?*"

I turned my mind off for a while, just putting one foot in front of the other, stick in hand, supporting my weight. I tried to think of nothing but getting out of those woods.

What seemed like hours passed. I heard the grumble of my stomach as it groaned for food. My tongue was dry. I had sucked on ice and snow along my trek, but it wasn't enough to curb my thirst. The darkness had begun to fade when what seemed like a vision appeared up ahead. It was a log cabin with a high, pitched roof and a small porch. On the cabin's side, grey stone stretched from the base of the cabin forming into a tall chimney atop the roof. Behind the cabin was a work shed with a gravel driveway between the cabin and its shed.

I hobbled, propelling my body in a forward motion in my attempt to reach my new destination.

Maybe they'll have a phone, I thought. *I can call for help! Oh, my gosh, I can't believe this is going to end!* As I neared the cabin, I noticed its dilapidation. The logs were peeling, exposing the brittle wood beneath the surface. Broken shards from the stone chimney had amassed in a heap on the ground below. It appeared, however, to be sturdy enough with its big, strong door.

I paused, wondering if I should knock or try the knob. It looked vacant. "At least I could escape the biting wind," I thought to myself.

As I ascended the cabin steps, the early morning sun spied through the trees, leaving haunting shadows across the cabin door. I jerked

back; repulsed, as a spider swung from its silken

fiber. It landed on the knob and crept up,

returning to complete its elaborate latticework.

Closing my eyes, I drew in a breath as I

hesitantly raised my fist to knock...

11

(Thirty Hours Missing)

Detective Silba leaned over her notes, intently studying their contents. *What is she doing?* Angie thought to herself. *Go find my daughter!*

Her stomach sank as the clock struck four and she became aware that her daughter had been gone for nearly a day and a half.

"Look, I know it hasn't been 48 hours," Angie began, "but my daughter's missing. Please go out there and find her before—"

"—we are doing everything we can," Detective Silba interrupted, addressing her plea. "The 48-hour waiting period is an urban myth. The department treats each situation on a case-by-case basis. Josie is our number one priority right now – that I can promise you."

Flipping her notepad to the next page, she questioned, "Now, Angie, can you tell me about Mr. James Fogel, Josie's father?"

"Jim and I met when I was eighteen. We got married, had Josie, and we separated about five years later. The divorce was final four years ago. He's no longer in the picture."

"You don't have any contact with him?" she asked.

"No, he was in and out of our lives...when I'd call him out on stuff, he'd bail. We tried to work things out when he kept comin' back around making promises about four years ago, just after I filed the divorce papers, if you'd believe that." Angie revealed.

Detective Silba scrawled in her notes. Biting the end of her pen, she asked, "And your youngest daughter, is she Eric's daughter?"

"No, no, Eric doesn't have his own kids. Em is Jim's daughter also. I got pregnant when we tried working things out four years ago or so. I wanted to believe he would change." She looked at the ground in shame.

"So what was the reason for the separation initially?"

Angie released a breath of air, blowing her bangs from her face. "His parents died in an automobile accident before we met– a drunk driver," she said, waving her hand in the air, recalling the tragedy. "He struggled with their death – always blames his problems on losing his parents when he was a kid. I tried to get him to go to counseling… God knows, I tried." She looked downward with tears in her eyes.

"I see," Detective Silba said, plainly.

"Jim has no other family. He said all the right things when we started dating. He made promises he couldn't keep. I was young and stupid and believed every word. But he was absent, even when he was in the house, he wasn't 'here.' He never was the settling down type. He wasn't a good provider—had no work ethic, and I had to think about Josie. He didn't have it in him to be a dad. He never even held her. You know, he wasn't even at the hospital when I had her? I didn't have it in me to continue living in that way, and after five years of his lies, absences, and our fighting, I asked him to leave. I finally came up with the money to file for divorce when Josie was almost nine," she stated with a sigh.

"But you reunited?" Detective Silba questioned, listening intently.

"Yes, four years ago, he started coming around after receiving the divorce papers. He got a job, and though he traveled a lot and lived outside of town, he acted like he'd grown up and changed. It seemed too good to be true. We never even told Josie that we were dating. I didn't want her to get her hopes up. I became pregnant. I confirmed the pregnancy and told Jim. He seemed really excited, or at least he feigned excitement," she recalled with fondness before biting her lower lip and bringing her hands up to her head.

"About a week or two later, he had found a buyer for his condo and was interviewing for a job all in the same week. He was overwhelmed and said he needed to take time while he went out of town for the interview to figure out what the next step was. Meanwhile, I was considering telling Josie that her dad wanted to start having a relationship with her again."

"What did you think that meant at the time?" Detective Silba wondered aloud.

"That he didn't know whether to take the new job and move as a family out of state or turn down the job and move here, in the home we once shared," she answered matter-of-factly. "It never occurred to me that he was having second thoughts…he put on such a good show, but when I didn't hear from him, I figured he made his decision and we weren't a part of it. About a month later, I went to the condo looking for him, only to find the new owners, no forwarding address; his car was gone. With his parents deceased and no siblings, I had nowhere to turn for answers." She paused for a moment while struggling for the right words. "We had been through the roughest time of our lives together. I wasn't interested in dragging Josie and a new baby through that a second time. I needed to let him go and live his life, and I, mine."

"I understand," Detective Silba said with comforting eyes. "How did Eric come into the picture?"

Angie struggled with the answer. While guarded, she complied, answering the question with, "He was a neighbor of ours," while pointing toward the window. "We didn't know him very well, but when I filed for divorce, Eric helped me with things around the house –you know, mowing the lawn, power washing the house. We dated a little bit, but it was not serious. I'm old fashioned. I wasn't interested in starting a serious relationship while still married, even though I had filed. When Jim came back in the picture, I broke it off with Eric and explained that I had to think of Josie and give this relationship a chance."

"And when Jim left, you rekindled your romance with Eric," Detective Silba deduced.

"No, not right away," Angie replied, locking eyes with Detective Silba, displeased in her assumption. "After Jim left, I was destroyed. Eric came around now and then, but I wasn't ready for another relationship. I had lost the love of my life for the second time. Even with his faults and instability, he was still the only love I ever knew. I didn't grow up in a stable home. My parents were divorced. My mom drank. My dad couldn't hold a job. I didn't know what a healthy relationship was. But Eric continued pursuing me until I finally told him about the pregnancy. He didn't come around for a few weeks—I figured that did it. Then he just showed up one day with a crib and a bunch of baby items, saying he thought I might need them. But it wasn't until Em was about six months old that we started dating again."

"Thank you for your candor, Angie. I know that wasn't easy," she recognized. "Are you aware of Jim's whereabouts today?"

"No, I have no idea. He hasn't contacted me. Like I said, I checked the condo, looked for his car, went to his former employer—nothing. I never even knew what company he was interviewing for. I got the signed divorce papers in the mail and that was it."

"And he doesn't have any family. No grandparents, aunts, uncles, cousins?" Detective Silba asked.

"No, when his parents died, he was alone. His grandparents died when he was a kid, and both of his parents were only-children, as well," she explained, adding, "He moved from home to home as a kid. I don't think he ever even lived with family."

"Ok, let's shift gears... Do you know if Josie met anyone new recently?"

"No, not that I know of," she replied. "She's pretty open with me."

"And what about boys, does she have a boyfriend?"

With her brow furrowed, Angie answered, "No, she doesn't really show interest in boys much at all. She's a really smart, somewhat quiet kid – incredibly responsible, almost to a fault."

"What do you mean by that – in what way?" she questioned.

"What I mean is; she is the type of kid who knows the rules and follows them. Where most 13-yr olds would be pushing limits, she helps around the house without asking. She takes care of her little sister when my hands are full. My daughter is one of the most level-headed kids I know," she recalled, looking down at the ground, the tears beginning to form.

"So, responsible beyond her age, is that right?" she concluded.

"Absolutely," Angie confirmed, nodding her head in agreement, adding "more than most, in fact. She has the ability to step into a situation and take charge if needed, yet will stand back and listen, happily taking direction, as well. She notices everything, and she has been that way since she was just a baby. Teachers report her to be the kid they can count on, even nominating her as hall monitor."

Detective Silba scribbled as Angie spoke, taking in her words, yet saying nothing.

"Detective Silba, she really is missing. This isn't a joke. It's not an attempt on her part to get attention. She didn't run away. *I implore you to take this seriously*," Angie pleaded as tears pricked at her eyes once again.

"I assure you, Mrs. McIntosh that we are doing everything we can. I know it seems like we are sitting around while your daughter is missing, but it is my job to first, eliminate family members. I hate to say it, but the closer an individual is to a child, the more likely they are involved. It is my duty to find her and figure out what happened. Part of that includes removing all the roadblocks. I know it seems cruel, but it's standard procedure. What you've told me leads me to believe that she is, in fact, missing, and Angie, I don't believe that you are involved, but I can't go on gut alone. I must thoroughly interview you, your husband, neighbors, friends, co-workers, teachers, janitors, coaches, and anyone with which she came into contact. All of these people are potential suspects. Now, that being said, you are right – we don't have time to waste. So, while I am analyzing the information you and your husband have shared with us, Detective Falcor is getting two or three hours of sleep. We will get –"

Angie shot up from her seat, her face flaming with rage.

"Sleep?! He's sleeping while Josie is out there somewhere freezing to death or being –" Angie choked on the words, "molested by some pervert?!" She seethed, venom spewing from her lips as she shouted.

"Angie, calm down. I understand this is difficult. We aren't sleeping through your case," she stood and with a wave of her hand, motioned Angie to follow her to the kitchen. "It's four o'clock in the morning and I am still here with you. Detective Falcor circulated the photo you submitted to us; spoke with the newspapers and local news channels. He's doing what he can. The office is the best place for him to be right now. He's simply resting up there, where he can be reached if news about Josie comes in. He had been on the job for over twenty-four hours prior to receiving your call, whereas I was not. I am here with you, working the case, and he is nearby. We are no good to Josie in a sleep-deprived fog. He has contacted the FBI. When they arrive in the morning, they will begin their investigation and conduct a search of the area. There are numerous behind-the-scenes steps to take before we are able to move forward. Once the FBI arrives, we will work for days straight with no breaks. He is preparing his body for that feat," Detective Silba explained while pouring two tall cups of black coffee, offering one to Angie.

She accepted the cup. "Thank you, I could use that," she said wrapping her fingers around the warm mug. "I know you are doing what you can. It's just – I just... just find her," she finished as her eyes glazed over with tears.

12

Upon knocking on the cabin door, I heard the crack of a twig behind me. Drawing in a breath and praying it was nothing, I turned.

The butt of the gun cracked against my skull. I stumbled backward, into the now open doorway, my eyes blurring the dark figure before me. Stumbling around, I fell into extended arms. Thick blood cascading from my open wound obstructed my view.

"Uhhhh," I groaned as a stabbing pain traveled through my neck. My legs gave out beneath me. I wanted to struggle—to fight. I was unable. I could not move. Through the blood, I watched as a syringe dropped to the floor.

"Whaddo you wan fruh me?" I slurred, gripping the person guiding me inside.

"Shhh!" a whisper advised. "Just do what he says."

"Shut up!" I heard my captor say, before hearing a smack of skin.

"Yes, sir," a meek whisper responded.

I was unable to move as my captors dragged me deeper into the cabin. My body became limp. I had no ability to stand, much less run. I tried to take in my surroundings, but by now, was unable to open my eyes. A door opened, exposing a damp, musty smell. *A basement*, I thought. For the first time, I realized I really might die here.

The tops of my feet dragged behind me, hitting each step as they hauled me down to the dank basement below. They hobbled with my heavy, unmanned body to what seemed like the farthest point. My captor readjusted his position, his arms beneath my underarms, wrapping them around my body.

He yelled, "Get the door!" With nothing but the light tap of feet, a second person navigated the room. As the door creaked, he gave more demands, "Restrain her," he yelled. I heard the cavernous echo of a chain moving against a concrete floor. In an instant, he threw me to the ground, where I lay in the position in which I was thrown, unable to resist. One of them slapped a cold metal restraint on one wrist. A moment later, the thick door clanged shut, locking behind me.

I cried, "Please! No!" but no sound escaped my throat. I broke down internally. Wailing, begging them to let me go, yet failing to make a sound as the drug pumping through my veins abducted both my mind and body.

13

(Four Days Missing)

"Thank you, Shawna," Angie said to Jessie's mom. Before ending the phone call, she added, "I assumed they would speak to everyone who comes into contact with our family. I appreciate you giving me the heads up."

Angie held on the phone for a moment before placing it on the hook. Knowing her reaction would be analyzed she drew in a large breath of air and turned in an attempt to remove any hint of anxiety.

"Where were we?" Detective Falcor questioned. "Oh, yes, I was just introducing Agent Martin of the FBI to you." She sat down, waiting for them to approach.

"You were about to tell me how you are going to find my daughter," she said, struggling to keep her tired eyes open.

A stout man looked at Angie, limping as he approached her. With dark brown hair and greying sideburns, Angie guessed he was about fifty. He unbuttoned the coat of his expensive suit before taking a seat in front of her. He put his glasses on as he raised the case file to his eyes to get a better look. He then leaned forward with his elbows on his knees, his glasses sliding down his nose. With his piercing eyes looking over the frames, he said, "When did your husband lose his job?"

"He still works for the freighter. His employer cut his hours off-and-on over the last six months." Noticing their puzzlement, she explained with a sigh, "Eric has been under review for fighting with co-workers, but he spoke with his boss and started working full time again. Things are good."

Detective Falcor and Agent Martin looked at each other before Agent Martin raised his glasses again, his mouth open, breathing loudly as he flipped through his notepad until he landed on the information he was looking for. He looked up and removed his glasses. Putting the stem to the corner of his mouth, he lightly shook the notepad in her direction saying, "I have it on good authority that he hasn't worked for at least three weeks." He didn't blink, with raised eyebrows above suspicious eyes, he waited for a response.

Angie eyes widened and her mouth hung agape. "What? What are you saying? Why would he lie to me about that?" she choked. She felt hot as her face flushed. With a furrowed brow she quietly said, "I don't understand," looking back and forth between them.

"Your husband didn't tell you he lost his job?" he questioned a second time.

"No. I knew nothing about it." She looked at Agent Martin, holding his gaze, firm in her answer. "Where has he been going every day? He's been coming and going at the same time every day. And things were improving financially for us."

"You say things were improving?"

"Yes, that's exactly what I'm saying," she confirmed as she stood affirming her statement by towering over the agent.

"Ok, that's all we need for now," Agent Martin said, as he rose from his seat. "We will want to speak with Mr. McIntosh again, as well."

"That's it? That's all you are going to say to me? What about Josie? Have you found anything?!" she exclaimed, chasing them as they headed toward the door.

Detective Falcor turned toward her. "Angie, we are doing everything we can. Search parties are out looking. We are working on getting a team together to begin dragging the lake," he said with an empathetic touch of her arm before exiting the home.

***

Angie turned the TV on, and upon seeing Josie's picture before her, she held her breath. The bottom of the screen scrolled saying,

Missing Child: Josie Fogel, 13, last seen Friday leaving her home in the Westchester neighborhood wearing jeans and a heavy purple coat.

Moments later, the news anchor filled the screen. "The 13-year-old went missing Friday afternoon as she walked just one-half of a mile

from home to meet a friend here at this park,"
she said, with an extended arm, indicating to the
park behind her. "Law Enforcement officials state
that Josie is one of two children born to Mrs.
Angie McIntosh and Mr. David Fogel. Detectives
are attempting to locate Josie's father, who has
not had contact with his ex-wife in almost four
years. Mrs. McIntosh is cooperating with
investigators. Mr. McIntosh, Josie's step-father, is
currently being questioned in the case, but is not
being named as a suspect at this time. Sources
tell us that Mrs. McIntosh and her former
husband, Mr. Fogel, were separated in 1998, but
during an attempt at reconciliation in 2002, Mrs.
McIntosh became pregnant with their youngest
daughter. Mr. Fogel left town and never returned,

leaving only the signed divorce papers filed months earlier. He left his ex-wife to raise the two girls on her own until she married Mr. McIntosh, a neighbor of the Fogel family, in 2004. Police urge anyone with information to contact them at the phone number listed at the bottom of the screen."

She turned the TV off and thought, *Can this really be happening?*

As she sifted through photos of Josie, she set aside four of her favorite images. She tapped her finger on each one while memories of her lost daughter flashed in her mind. Blinking back tears, she thought, *I never would have expected to choose one of these happy memories as the photo for a Missing Child Flyer*.

A half-hour later, Eric arrived home. She said nothing, but her anger was apparent. She flipped through photos, forcefully slamming one after the other on the counter.

He put his hand over hers, saying, "it'll be okay."

She withdrew her hand and waved him aside. Her steely eyes pierced his with uncontrolled fury. She turned her back to him and put her hands to her forehead. Her hair flew as she turned on her heels to face him once again.

With a wagging finger, she yelled, "Do you have anything you want to tell me?" Eric said nothing.

"Did you think I wouldn't find out?" she asked, incredulously. "What was your plan – how did you think this would end?"

"I didn't know how to tell you," he said, looking down.

"So you lied? You acted like you were leaving for work every day and going God knows where." The silence was deafening. Angie looked at Eric, waiting for a reply. When he said nothing, she said, "Don't you know how bad this looks? Now, you are hiding this horrible secret. The FBI suspects you. If you didn't have anything to do with—"

"Woah—*If?*" he said. Disturbed, he raised his hand to his face, scratching at the overgrowth from days of no sleep or showers.

"I thought I knew you better than this, Eric, but what am I supposed to think? My daughter is missing, and I find out for the last three weeks or more, you've not only lied about losing your job, but also about where you were going day to day. And even when Josie goes missing, you still don't think it's important enough to tell me," she challenged, clearly waiting for his response.

"There wasn't a good time. I didn't know what to say or how to say it. I wanted to focus my energy on finding her, Angie. I love her, too, you know," he declared, with his hands outstretched, begging for her trust.

"Do you? Because for the last year, I've felt like we've been nothing but a burden to you," she admitted.

"I know I made you feel like that, and I'm sorry. It wasn't you. It was all me. I wasn't handling myself right at work. With the money, and the fighting, and the loans, I couldn't do it all on my own," he conceded, with his shoulders down and his chest deflated.

Angie knew they were having financial problems, but the word loans troubled her. What did he mean by *loans?* Were there more bills of which she was unaware? What had he gotten himself – the whole family – into?

She looked at him with tears in her eyes. "Tell me everything."

"I owe money—a lot of money," he admitted, as she looked him in the eye.

Pounding her fists into his chest, she screamed, "You did this! You put our family in danger. You put my daughter at risk! You could get her killed!"

She pushed him away in disgust as he interrupted her, saying, "No, Angie. He'll come after *me* for it, not you, and not the girls," he insisted.

"They *did* go after you, Eric! This is how they will get to you! If you had brought this up to begin with, we'd be that much closer to finding her by now!"

He grabbed her wrists, forcing her to look at him. "We'll find her."

She broke from his grip and said, "You better," before stepping around him and out the door.

14

I will do whatever it takes to get him to keep me alive. With each day that I'm alive, I have a chance of returning to my family. I will do this for them.

I had been lying there for what seemed like hours. I could finally move my fingers and toes. When I woke, I remembered wishing it had been a nightmare. I prayed I would wake up in my bed, with Em next to me smiling.

Em! I thought to myself. *She must be so upset that I'm not there.* Tears began to form, but I blinked them back, willing myself to be strong. I knew if I let my emotions go, I would die here. I needed to be smart. Maybe someone would take pity on me. Was it possible there was an ally in the home, I wondered, remembering the voice telling me to listen to my abductor.

I listened intently to my surroundings – Nothing. I wondered how deep this basement was. The door sounded strong when it clanged shut. I attempted to lift my head, but I was still groggy from the drugs. I willed myself to stay awake, but my eyes were so heavy.

A whispered voice said, "It's okay." I froze, but opened my eyes, hoping I could tell where the voice came from. It was dark.

"Who's there?" I whispered, but there was no answer. I allowed my heavy eyes to close once again.

Hours later, I awoke to the sound of the turning of heavy locks. I could now move my whole body, so I scurried into the corner, as far as the chain would stretch. As the door opened, I squinted to see, but could only see the silhouette of a man. He slid a plate across the concrete floor. On it was a piece of bread slathered in ketchup. He then threw a thermos in my direction. Before I could tell him it was out of reach, he shut the door. A light went on. The lurid room was cold and small. It was concrete from floor to ceiling. There was a cot on the other side. The light was a dim bulb attached to a wire that traveled up to the ceiling where it anchored to a cemented-in-place steel rod. The wire followed the rod to the edge of the room where it disappeared through a cavity in the wall adjacent to the door. The door climbed from floor to ceiling. It was a thick, heavy door, seemingly made of steel. It contained a small window in the center of the door that was capable of being opened and closed.

As I looked around, I realized I was not the first person to be here. Marks adorned the wall next to me. Hash marks indicating the number of days someone had been imprisoned here. I wondered if they ever made it out and suddenly felt a pang of sympathy for my previous cell owner. *Where had they gone? Did they get away? Did they die in here?*

I ate the sandwich, stuffing the bread and its condiment in my mouth with force. Its sogginess slithered down my throat. Although I shivered in disgust, my stomach ached for more. I figured it had been two days since I had eaten. The saltiness of the ketchup left me parched. I stretched for the thermos. I extended my arm from its imprisoned wrist and shot my leg out in an attempt to kick the thermos closer to me.

I flipped over on my stomach stretching my arm as far as I could, sensing the restraint biting into my flesh. "Uggghhh," I groaned, willing my body to elongate farther, pointing my toe, swiping it to the left. *Chink, flumpf, Chink,* it rolled about 6 inches closer to me. "Uhhhh." Again, I forced myself to pull. The sharp edge of the cuff dug in and drew blood on my wrist. I groaned, heaving my body as far as I could. I swiped again at the thermos, managing to collect it momentarily before moving it 6 inches back to where it was to begin with. With the blood moving down my arm now, I put the pain out of my mind. I took in a deep breath, and with motivational tears, stretched my arm first, then my waist. Then, feeling the bullet wound ache in resistance, I fought the pain. I pushed to the limit and swung my leg as far as I could, using my foot once again to propel the thermos closer.

This attempt did it. I cried as I opened the thermos. My first victory.

***

There was nothing to do but think, cry, and sleep. I drank about one-fourth of the thermos, forcing myself to use some on my leg and leave some for later.

A while later I called out, "Hello!? I have to go to the bathroom!"

The peephole in the door slid open and a pair of eyes peered in. "I have to pee. Can you help me?" They weren't the dark, sinister eyes I was faced with before. These were different. They were sad, empathetic eyes.

"He's not here. I can't get in. Look around –
is there a bottle or anything you can use?" the
voice whispered.

I looked around, and although the light was
still on, it was very dim. "I –I think there may be
a milk jug or something in the corner, but I don't
know if I can reach it," I answered.

"Just a minute," the voice said. With that,
the slot was closed and he was gone. I became
fixated on the peephole, willing it to open again. I
shimmied toward the corner in an attempt to
reach the jug. A surge of pain spread through my
wrist. I looked down and for the first time, I
realized how much the restraint had lacerated my
hand. I examined the cuff. It was sharp, as if it
had been filed to a point in order to foil any

escape plan. I took the half-full thermos and poured a small amount over my wounds. The water spread over the dried blood, washing it away. The wounds hurt, but they were not deep.

Several minutes went by before the slot opened and once again, the somber eyes appeared. "I'm going to try to use this stick to push the jug closer to you. Get ready to catch it," the voice said. A broomstick appeared in the opening and slowly moved down toward the floor nowhere near the jug. Swiping it back and forth, he said, "I can't reach unless I use my fingertips, but if I drop this, I'm dead." As the stick retreated through the opening, the voice said, "I'm sorry."

"Wait!" I pleaded. "Please, try again. I really have to go," I added trying to buy time.

"I'm sorry," the voice said. The eyes were back now, gazing through the opening at me.

"Can you push it through to me?" I suggested, in a hopeful voice. I'll use it to get the jug and give it right back you – he'll never know."

"I don't know…" I heard the voice reply.

"Ok, I can hold it. But please don't leave. What's your name?" I asked, in an attempt to gain trust. There was no answer. "Mine is Josie," I said. "I want to get home to my family. Did he take you, too?"

With that, the voice disappeared and the peephole closed. I cried out, sobbing, "Why are you doing this? Pleeease! I need to get home to my family!" I knew it was no use, for no one could hear me. The voice was as scared as I was. It was such a hushed whisper; I could not tell if it was a boy or a girl. I knew it was someone young, possibly even my age. I wondered if they were kept here and free to move about, or if they grew up here. I closed my eyes praying for a rescue.

15

(Five Days Missing)

Cameras and microphones stared back at her as she spoke. "It's time for Josie to come home. We love her," she said shaking. "Her little sister asks for her every night. This is where she belongs. Please let her come home," Angie stepped away, unable to finish as she sobbed.

Eric spoke up, "Please, if you know anything, call the police. If you saw anything, even the slightest thing, please tell somebody. Something you might think was nothing, could be something. This is our only hope—the public is our only hope." While still sobbing, Angie descended the risers and fell into the arms of her friends and family with Eric following behind her with his head hung low.

Police Sergeant Ackroid took the podium next. "We are doing everything we can to find Josie. As time goes by, however, we become farther and farther from finding her. Please contact the police if you have any information."

"Sergeant Ackroid! –Angela Dillon with *The Journal*," a reporter broke in, raising her arm up in the air, commanding his attention. "What have you done up to this point to find Josie?"

"Let me defer to Detective Falcor, lead Detective on the case, and Agent Martin of the FBI." He stepped aside, making room for the two men.

Placing his case file on the podium, Detective Falcor began, "Search and rescue dogs were used to determine if blood was found in or around the home and have yet to turn up anything indicating an altercation occurring at home. Search dogs lost her scent at the corner of Countryside Drive in the Westchester neighborhood, near Jennings Rd. This is less than a mile from the home. This leads us to believe that she may have gotten into a vehicle there." He took a deep breath before continuing, "The only piece of evidence we found was a purple glove, believed to be hers that was found on Countryside Drive. We are treating this as abduction. Crime Scene Units are currently testing the glove to confirm that it is Josie's. While we have not yet ruled out family and friends, we are leaning in the direction of a stranger abduction."

Reporters began talking over each other with more questions. The loudest stepped forward, "Robert Mulrooney with ABC News," he said, "Have the 14 registered sex-offenders living in a 30-mile radius of the home been interviewed?"

"Yes, we have done extensive interviewing of all neighbors, including the 14 registered sex-offenders, all of which have iron-clad alibis. While it is important to look at registered sex-offenders, it is just as important not to overlook those with clean records," he added.

"While we are scaling back our search operations in the woods behind Josie's home, we will be dragging the pond just two miles from the home tomorrow, weather permitting. We are not giving up. We are sifting through the hundreds of tips that have come in, as well as focusing harder on specific areas," he stated. "Thank you for your time. And again, please report anything you think might be important. What may seem like the smallest tip may be enough to bring this little girl home," he concluded.

16

I awoke to the clanging of the steel door. It must have been late, as there was no light streaming in other than the dim indoor lighting behind their silhouettes. I sat up, trying to make sense of my surroundings. I could see shadows approaching.

"Get in there, boy," the man said before he shoved the boy through the door. He tripped and nearly landed on me. He picked himself up and said "I am," to the man.

I looked at him with questioning eyes. He looked back and mouthed, "I'm sorry." I knew he wanted to help so I gave a quick nod of the head, so slight it was undetected by my captor. I looked at him again feeling a sense of familiarity. He looked down, avoiding my gaze.

"Clean 'er up!" the man yelled, noticing my urine soaked clothes. I unbuttoned my jeans and slid them down, removing them from my body with one hand. He gave me a wet towel, which I used to sop up the urine.

"I called for help. Held it as long as I could," I uttered, meekly.

The man ignored me as he threw a sponge at the boy. A pail sloshed nearby as the man used his foot to push it toward us. His voice bellowed,

"Clean it up, boy! Whatchyou think, it's gonna clean itself? And then get 'er dressed!"

"Yes, sir," the boy answered.

I scooted over so he could clean the floor and immediately noticed the bruises on the back of his neck and arms. He was a thin boy with dark, shaggy hair that fell over his face. I wanted to talk to the boy, but the man stood eyeing us. He was talking to himself, grumbling incoherently.

The boy was taking his time cleaning. I suspected he liked the company of someone else enough to clean pee off the floor. I glanced up and saw the man looking away. I raised my wrist and showed the boy the cuts. He grimaced and looked into my eyes as if to say something without words.

He raised the gown and said, "She needs the cuff removed before I can put this on her," with his eyes still on mine." The man came in and put a knife to my throat. His tenebrous eyes pierced my soul. "Move and I'll kill you," he said while giving the boy the key to my restraint. I didn't move.

Moments later, I pulled my hand up to my fissured wrist in protection. The man backed up toward the door opening, calling to the boy, "Hurry up. We gotta make some money today."

The boy finished cleaning, and with fear in his eyes, he slipped my shirt over my head keeping his eyes on mine, and slipped the gown over my body.

I wished I could talk to him. I opened my mouth ready to whisper, but when I looked up, the man stood above us and yanked the boy out of the room by his neck and threw him through the door. I cringed and said *sorry* with my eyes as the door slammed between us.

Little time went by when the door opened again. The boy came in with the man following close behind carrying a whip. It was dark, but I could see that the boy was naked. He had lash marks across his chest. He turned toward the man, and breathlessly said, "Please." His back matched his chest, the lash marks crisscrossing. The man took a step forward, raising the whip before striking the boy. He fell to the ground and allowed a howl to escape his lips. My kidnapper stood behind him clutching a blazing white light with a red blinking light. He placed it on a tripod. The boy looked at me and brought his mouth to my ear. He whispered, "I'm sorry, I'm so sorry. It'll be over soon, I promise. You'll be okay."

I felt wet droplets fall to my cheek. I looked past him still unsure of what was about to happen and saw a man standing, smiling over us.

Picking the boy up by his hair, he threw him to the ground behind him. My captor looked at the stranger and held his hand out, rubbing his thumb against his four remaining fingers.

"I already paid you!" the stranger exclaimed, bracing his beastly body, ready for a fight. I glanced past them with fear in my eyes, looking for the boy. He mouthed, *I'm sorry*, as the tears streamed down his face.

With a look of anger in my captor's eyes, I hear the click of a gun hammer. "You paid for a girl. You didn't pay for a young 'un. You want her, you pay more."

There are more of us here? I thought to myself. *Where? How many? Who?* I looked to the boy, willing him to read my mind. All he did was shake his head as he lowered his eyes to the ground.

"How much? I've already paid a thousand. What more do I gotta pay?" The strange man grumbled.

"She's worth five grand. She's fresh, if you know what I mean." My captor smirked at the man while wiggling his eyebrows, "I gotta have four K more."

"Fresh? Hmmm. Sounds nice," the man said while bringing his hand to his groin. He continued to look at me, piercing me with his cold, dark eyes. His smile sickened me as he rubbed himself.

As he reached around to the back of his pants my captor got jumpy. He raised the gun as the stranger held his hand up and said, "Hold up, man. I'm just getting the money. She looks like a fine, fresh piece." He looked down at me and licked his lips saying, "You ready for a man, little girl?"

The words wouldn't come. As my breath choked in my throat, I began shaking.

My captor took the money and set up the camera behind them.

Before my captor left, the stranger said, "Hey, your ad said you'd tape the flower without the thorns...so that means I'm not in this video, right?"

"Yeah, yeah man. We'll blur you out. But we'll give you access so you can watch 'er scream over and over."

As the steel door slammed, I squeezed my eyes shut screaming internally as the man approached.

17

The door slammed behind them as I curled into a fetal position, letting the tears stream down my cheeks. I curled my arms around my stomach, fighting the urge to vomit.

I thought about the last several days and vowed to get out of this place. My abductor was stealing my soul. He was taking everything from me, but it was time to stop him. It may take me seven days, seven months, or seven years, but I was determined to get out of this alive.

He had forgotten to restrain me, so I was able to move around the room. I walked along the walls, feeling them for cracks. Rubbing my hands across the concrete, which was smooth in some places and rough in others, I found no openings in the first wall. I continued on, feeling my way across the next wall. When I came to the door, I felt the edge for gaps. It was solid. I kept hunting, careful to keep an ear out for his approach.

Along the last wall, there were words carved into the cement next to the hash marks. I couldn't make them out. I wanted a connection— someone who had been through this to speak to me from beyond. I hoped she had escaped, but I knew better. At the base of the writing were chipped pieces of concrete. I gathered them into a pile and swept them into the palm of my hand and looked around for a place to keep them. I made my way to the cot on the other wall and temporarily placed them beneath the cot's frame.

I felt the frame of the bed, looking for anything I could use as a weapon, while at the same time, looking for a place to hide the shards. A mildew-laden fabric sheath filled with cotton material lay on the frame. My fingers crept along the edge of the frame. I lifted the frame to find an opening under the leg at the base of frame. I poked my finger in. Perfect! I placed the stones up into the leg of the frame, holding my finger against the bottom as I laid the frame back down on the ground.

After experiencing the most horrible day
since my abduction, I felt a sense of renewed
hope in this smallest of triumphs. Continuing to
examine the bed, I decided to lift the other three
legs. The next leg had the original covering, not
permitting items to be hidden underneath. I
checked the next one, which bent at the base,
again, not allowing me the additional hiding place
for which I had hoped. I arrived at the last leg
and felt something at its base. I was unable to lift
it much for fear of the stone shards clanging
against the floor on the other end as I raised it. I
moved back to the first leg, removing the stones
carefully and quietly. I went back to the fourth
leg and pulled the leg up higher. I attempted to
grasp the item inside, but my fingers were unable

to fit. I stuck my pinkie finger up into the metal and attempted to slide the object down.

Swiveling my pinkie around to get a better hold on it, I pulled down slowly, careful not to lose it. *Ah, ha! Success!* I thought to myself. I looked at it. Paper.

I unrolled the scroll to read,

> 1.   *You found this. Good job.*
>
> 2.   *Do what he says.*
>
> 3.   *He will give you water every other day. Make it last.*
>
> 4.   *I'm sorry.*

It didn't say much. Whoever wrote the note knew I would be here before I arrived. Was it the boy? A previous prisoner?

I threw the note under the bed as I heard the peephole slide open and the blue eyes peered through.

"You have to be quicker than that," the voice said. "Next time, sit on the other side of the bed, facing the other way so he can't see you if he comes.

I got up and approached the door, praying he wouldn't leave.

"Is he going to kill me?" I asked.

He looked down. "Just do what he says," he pleaded. "I gotta go. He'll be back any minute."

"Wait. I don't want to be in here alone," I started to cry. "Please."

"Come closer. I brought you something," he said.

I raised my hand to the window, and he placed a wad of paper into my palm. I opened it and looked. "Band-Aids," I said out loud. I looked up as the peephole closed.

I sat down and opened the thermos, pouring the water over my wounds. When dry, I placed a Band-Aid over the leg wound. I left my wrist unbandaged so as not to attract attention from my kidnapper.

At that moment, I pledged to do whatever it took to get home. It was then that I began to plan my escape. Though it would be long and I would have to be patient, I knew I would make it out alive.

18

I quietly removed one stone from beneath
the leg at the base of the bed frame. As I carved
my 18th hash-mark on the floor beyond the bed,
tears fell. I was unsure whether I was counting
the days I had been missing or the number of
times I had been violated by various strange men
he had brought into the dungeon. I left the
stones and climbed onto the filthy bed, curling
into the fetal position, craving the comfort of my
own bed at home. I sobbed, thinking of my mom

and Em, and wishing my dad had never left, wondering if he knew I was missing.

When the tears ceased, anger followed. Every time the boy approached, my evil captor following behind with camcorder in hand, I knew what was to come. He whispered in my ear each time he uncuffed me, begging me to just do what they say. I felt betrayed, wondering how he could let this happen to me. As his tears cascaded down his cheeks, I knew he was as sad and disturbed as I was, yet my anger grew. Each time he came to me with the recorder, a man would follow. *Didn't he know what they were doing to me?*

Exhausted from tears of sadness and anger, I allowed my eyes to close. I dreamt about Mom and Em. We used to go to the park all the time. When I woke up, I longed to smell flowers and hear birds sing. Moments later, the window at the center of the heavy door slid open. The boy snuck a roll through the small window in the door. I grasped at the roll when it hit the ground, starving after eating only bread with ketchup, canned tuna, and oatmeal throughout my imprisonment.

He whispered through the window, sensing my anger, "I would hate me, too." He looked down as I backed up, and onto the bed. When I didn't respond, he continued, "He whips me when I refuse, and if I still refuse he brings people to me… makes me do stuff with them," he admitted.

Without meeting his eyes, I said, "why don't you just leave?"

"Where would I go? No one would believe me if I told them," he answered, exasperated. "Besides, I will go to jail – he'll tell the police I'm the one that does it. He even has proof with the videos."

"But you haven't touched me like that. There's nothing on video with you!" I screamed, trying to convince him.

"But I've been on video before—before you," he said quietly.

My mouth formed an "O" as I sat down on the cot. "You did that to other girls?"

"When I was younger, the guy he works for made me."

"There's another man?" I squealed, "How many?"

"It's a big deal. I'm serious. I'll go to jail," he said with fear.

"Not if you go to the police yourself!" I exclaimed as I approached the window. I could see he was shaking. That evil man had stricken him with fear so deep that the boy believed everything he said. I treaded lightly, lowering my voice. "The police will know that you didn't want to do it. They will see the videos and know that he forced you. They'll see the marks on your chest and back!"

"No, I can't. He takes care of me. He'll kill me if I ever tried to leave or call someone. That's why we are out here in the middle of nowhere," he added. "I don't even go to school; he tells people he homeschools me. I don't see anyone else; I don't talk to anyone else unless he is by my side. You're the only friend I have."

My heart dropped to my stomach at the word 'friend.' Could he really think I was his friend? He kept me here, held captive. Despite the fact that it was not what he wanted, he did not free me. "I can't be your friend," I said, almost feeling guilty.

"I'm trying to help you," he said, trying to be convincing. "I know what I've done to you is wrong. I wish I didn't have to. I'm sorry," he said, before adding, "I left you the note; I gave you hints to help you survive in here. It's all I know how to do."

Ignoring his explanation, I asked, "Don't you miss your mom and dad? Don't you wish they would come and rescue you? Don't you ever want to get back to them?" I asked incredulously.

"He *is* my dad," he answered sadly before shutting the window.

I returned to carving hash marks in the ground, as it gave me something to do to pass the time. Feeling the side of the stone, I realized it was developing a sharp edge. At that moment, I decided to grind the largest of the stones into a sharp point. Fearful I would fail to hear the door, I only allowed myself a short time to work on this project. It would take a long time to develop a point that would work the way I had hoped. I dedicated myself to creating that point, beginning with the first, largest stone. I rubbed the stone against the concrete with fierceness, creating a cloud of dust in its wake. After ten minutes, I stopped, returning to the roll I had gotten from the boy. I had hidden pieces of it, hoping the ability to eat small amounts throughout the day would prevent me from getting so hungry. I ate two small pieces, allowing them to dissolve on my tongue, wishing I had more to eat. I forced myself to resist eating more, and instead opted for a swig of the thermos. His note had been right. The man gave water every other day. I was able to make it last; knowing this routine helped immensely. While I did not have nearly enough to keep my thirst at bay, I was able to gulp water after eating the soggy ketchup sandwich or the can of tuna thrown my way, both of which were salty, perpetuating my thirst.

Regardless of my anger, I allowed myself to thank the boy for the hints he wrote, for visiting me, and for bringing me Band-Aids and extra food. I was thankful but had not yet forgiven.

19

(Three Weeks Missing)

"Eric, when did you realize that this might be related to the money you owe?" Detective Silba asked.

"I didn't until Angie asked me if I realized this was my fault."

With the stem of her glasses between her teeth, she eyed him warily. "Can you tell me about James Fogel?" she asked, with a hint of knowing in her voice.

"What do you want to know?" Eric replied, his eyes shifting away from Detective Silba's.

"I mean, we know you've been in contact with him. Does Angie know this?" She looked at him, holding his gaze, letting him know she knew more than she let on.

"I'd only talked to him a handful of times before the last couple of years, and yes, I told her everything this morning. That is why I called you. I didn't know what I was getting myself into, I swear!" Eric exclaimed.

"Why did James leave?" she asked, while jotting down notes.

"He didn't want the family life. He never wanted to be a dad. Everything Angie tells you about him is what she wanted to believe. He told her what she wanted to hear, and she refused to see the truth." Eric looked down at his hands before adding, "I waited for him to leave. It was inevitable. He put up a good façade, but there's a lot that Angie doesn't know."

"Like What?" Detective Silba inquired, crossing her legs so Eric could see her tanned thigh, hoping to see if there was a hint of interest to gauge his character.

Eric's gaze followed along her legs but he quickly caught himself. "Jimmy acted like the perfect guy on the outside to people who didn't know him. I caught him in some lies and confronted him. He agreed to leave Angie alone if I kept his secrets."

"What secrets were those?"

"Like, he was never raised by his parents—never even knew them. The supposed accidental death of his parents was a way to placate Angie for his erratic behavior," he said, while placing air quotes around the word accidental. "I found out that they were drug dealers. His dad killed his mom in a fit of jealousy and went to prison. He died a few years later. He was stabbed in a yard fight. Angie believed his lies. She was working, and he wanted a free ride. He stuck around until she finally got fed up and filed for separation."

Detective Silba continued writing, occasionally glancing up at Eric. "Why didn't you tell Angie about his past?"

"I threatened to. I told him if he didn't tell her, I would. But in truth, I didn't want to hurt her. I figured what she didn't know wouldn't hurt her since at this point, they were already separated; divorce seemed inevitable. A few years later, he called my bluff and showed up again claiming to want Angie back. Then, when I heard about Angie getting pregnant, I told Jimmy to get out of town—to let her live her life."

"And he just agreed to that?" the detective asked.

"Well, the loans that I told Angie about weren't really loans at all. Jimmy said he'd leave them alone if I gave him money to get out of town. I did. He gave her the story about a new job and left the next day."

"He just left? Without saying anything?" she asked.

"Yeah. She waited around for a while, but then he sent the divorce papers, so she decided she was done with his antics."

"And you started coming around…" she trailed, waiting for his response.

"I waited a while to get back in the picture because I didn't want to be the second choice. About six months later, I brought over some stuff to help out with the baby. Jimmy hadn't shown his face in a while."

"—In a while? So, you had seen him during this time? Did you tell Angie?" she questioned.

He looked down shaking his head. "No. It was easier to live our lives with her believing he was gone for good. But, he would come back every few months demanding more; saying he has people doing work for him that he's gotta pay. Every time he would demand more, he would show up at my work threatening to hurt Angie or the girls. These appearances were getting noticed by management, so the last time he showed up, I refused."

Glad to see that Eric got on task quickly after crossing her long legs, detective Silba felt a sense of honesty in his words. *He really does love Angie and the girls*, she thought. Signs of truth were coming through, allowing her to get to the bottom of the missing ex-husband.

"When did you start to suspect that Jim had something to do with Josie's disappearance?" Detective Silba asked.

"I really didn't until you brought it up. I knew he kept telling me I owed him money and that one way or another I'd pay, but I didn't think he'd hurt his own daughter!" Eric stood, his emotions pouring out as he pounded his fists on the paneling beside him. "He always acted like I owed him for letting me have his family. Yet he didn't want anything to do with them anyway."

"I think that's all for now, Eric," she said as she rose to leave. With one hand on the door, she turned, "Can you tell me when the last time you saw Jimmy was?"

Eric's fist rose to his forehead as he answered, "I saw him last week. I've seen him regularly for the last few weeks. I should have said something," he added. "I just didn't know how to tell Angie. All the problems we've had lately – my job, our fighting, it all comes down to him."

She stepped away from the door, taking a step toward him, leading him to the kitchen as she set her satchel on the counter, pulling her notepad back out.

"How is that?" she asked inquisitively. "Has he threatened you?"

"Yes," Eric answered truthfully. "The problems I've had at my job are 'cause Jimmy kept coming up to my place of employment. He won't leave me alone, saying I owe him money since he agreed to leave town." He pounded his fist on the counter before offering, "He even took my car, saying it was for collateral. I made up a story of someone borrowing my car so as not to worry Ang."

"Do you know where Jimmy is now? Or where he can be reached?" Detective Silba faced Eric; pen poised to write.

Somberness crossed his features as he shook his head, defeat creeping into his eyes.

20

The hash marks revealed over four weeks in the dungeon, although I was unsure how long it had really been for sure. The time blended together. I marked the concrete each time he brought something for me to eat, which usually seemed to be once per day. Rarely did I get anything other than the ketchup-laden bread or occasional can of tuna.

My days were spent sharpening the stone, waiting for the opportunity to use it. With nothing else but scraps here and there from the boy, I was growing thin. My leg hadn't quite healed over, probably because of malnutrition.

Sliding my finger over the point of the stone, I decided today would be the day I would gain my freedom. The problem was that this day turned out to be the day I wanted it all to end, wishing for death over release.

***

I heard the door clang as it opened. I parted my eyes, waiting to be blinded by the light streaming in. It was him, with a pail of water.

"Get up," he directed. "You smell like shit, and I can't have that."

I crept off the cot, eyeing him closely. He yanked at my arms, tying them tightly behind my back. Pouring the freezing water over my body, he used a rough brush over my delicate, cold skin. I cried out before feeling his hand strike my cheek. As I stumbled backward, I could see the fire in his eyes. It was time. If I didn't get out now, I wouldn't get out alive. I went at him slamming my small, frail body into his. As he threw me to the ground, I saw stars. Opening my eyes, searching frantically for my stone, I scooted rapidly toward the cot, sensing it from behind as my fingers swept the floor behind me. His hand gripped my ankle and pulled me back over the rough concrete toward him. I kicked with all my might, fighting for my life. He grabbed my leg where the bullet wound still oozed, causing a painful moan to escape my lips. He began punching my face. Spitting blood and seeing stars, I knew it was now or never. As I struggled to free my wrists from the ties, I shuffled toward the cot. I could no longer see out of my left eye as it swelled up. I looked at him. With a smirk on his face, he moved toward me. I gripped the stone in my hand and held it tight, knowing I wouldn't be able to use it being tied up, but not willing to let it go. He picked me up by my hair, forcing me to my feet.

With my good eye, I glanced behind him at the open door, seeing the boy in the corner. My eyes pleaded for him to help me, to just give me a head start. He was shaking. He was as petrified as I was, as he held his breath preparing for a fight. With a look of fear, he mouthed, "Run!" I nodded to him.

At that, my captor turned and met the shovel the boy swung at his face. For an instant he was off balance. I ran, telling the boy to run with me, pushing his back ahead of me.

I turned back to close the door behind me and watched as my captor barreled through the big door. With blood pouring down his face, he looked angry and determined, but unsteady. Running through several doors and around the obstacles, I ran to a set of stairs. I looked up and saw the boy coming at me with scissors.

With my mouth open wide, fearing he'd changed his mind, he yelled for me to turn

around. I turned and he released the ties. In an
instant I was free. "GO!" I yelled as I saw his
burly father stumble through the opening. Lifting
his arm in aim, I heard a shot as I scurried up
the stairs. As the spray of bullets riddled the
rickety stairs, I covered my head as I ran in
flight. At the top of the stairs, I turned left,
following the boy as we ran. At the front door, he
stopped as he unlocked the 4 locks that secured
the prison from the outside. We darted through
the door, clearing the porch in a giant leap. I ran
into the woods without looking back. Once
beyond the cover of trees, I stopped to catch my
breath. My body ached. The pain, though surging
through my weakened muscles, did not impede

my speed, thanks to the adrenaline coursing through my body.

The boy looked at me. "Go up this way; you'll find a creek. It's frozen, but some flowing areas may have water. There's a large tree – you can't miss it. It looks like a pitchfork. It was hit by lightning and there's a hole in the side. When you find –"

"Wait. You're not coming?" I looked at him in awe, questioning his decision. "Why would you go back there? He'll kill you for what you've done."

"I don't know anyone else or anywhere else to go," he replied. "He'll beat me, but he won't kill me." He looked down, ashamed. "I don't know any other way. If I go back, he'll beat me long enough to give you time to get away. If you can just get to the tree—"

"—Just run with me. Go with me! I can get you help! You don't need to live like this," I cried. As angry as I had been at him, I longed for his freedom as I did my own. I pleaded with my eyes, urging him to come with me. "I don't think I can make it on my own," I admitted. "I need someone to help me find the way. I don't have it in me after all this. But we don't have time to talk about it," I said. "We either need to go, or you need to go back, but I'm heading out now."

I turned on my heels and started up the hill. The wind cut like a chilled axe. I had no meat on my bones to keep me warm. Fearing I would die out in the cold woods, I knew that was better than at the hands of my abductor. I was at that point. I would rather die in the woods than go back to that nightmare of a reality.

As I glanced back, I saw the boy shift his weight in my direction. Gripping the trees on the hill, he joined me at the top.

"No second thoughts," I said as we climbed over the hill.

21

I ran until my legs couldn't carry me any farther. I felt a firm grip on my arm coaxing me to keep going. I jerked away, fear entering my mind as I imagined my captor dragging me back to the dungeon. As I looked up, I saw the boy again and knew it was real. We had gotten away.

I cried out, "I can't!"

Responding, he took my face in his hands and forced my eyes to lock on his. "You can and you will. We didn't just go through all that for nothing."

"But look at my feet," I sobbed, looking down and my bloodied, frozen, blue toes. With just a gown covering my shivering body, I knew I would only last another hour or two.

"Ok, just a minute," he said as he led me to a nearby tree with a thick trunk that grew upwards into three points, like a pitchfork. Guiding me to the other side, he sat me down on one of the roots traveling outward from the base. With my teeth chattering, he blew into his palms before placing his hands over my toes. His hair hung in his eyes as he glanced upward through the strands.

"We will get you home. I promise," he said, before removing his own shoes and placing them on my feet. I looked up into those dark eyes, recognizing the meek, shy boy for the first time, but not saying anything.

With his lips slightly curving upward, letting me know it would be okay, he jumped up and reached deep inside a hole in the tree. He pulled out a satchel. Opening it revealed a blanket, which he used to wrap around my shoulders. For the first time, I smiled, my eyes glistening as the cold wind chilled against my face. He pulled open a bag and pulled out a bottle of water before placing four rolls in my hands.

I set three of the rolls on the plastic bag, noting boxes of raisins inside. "Dessert," he said with a grin.

Taking the fourth roll in my hand, I broke it, smiling at his attempt at a joke.

I struggled with my feelings for the next 15 minutes. Barely speaking, we sat together, eating and drinking our water, and trying to stay warm under the blanket.

Finally, I broke the silence, "When did you do all this?"

"One day last week, he forgot to lock my cage—"

"Your cage?" I asked, incredulously.

"Yeah," he said, looking down. "When he was home, I could be out, but when he left, he locked me up. About a month or two ago, I noticed that he kept forgetting to lock it. He was drinking more and more, and I would go in the cage when I knew he was leaving, hoping he would keep forgetting to lock it. I knew that he was going to take another girl, so on the days he would forget, I started thinking about how I could help her—I mean, you. I went into the basement and wrote the note I left for you."

"So you knew I was going to be there? How many other –"

"Four—" he interrupted himself. "You're the fourth."

"I'm the fourth," I repeated out loud, my voice trailing.

Avoiding my statement, he continued, "Last week, I started collecting things I thought could help if we ever got you out of here." He pulled a piece of paper out of his pocket, unrolling it while adding, "I drew this to help you find this tree where I hid everything." He passed the paper to me and opened the next bag. "I have matches, but don't use them until you get farther away,"

"I'm not leaving you!" Looking at him dumbfounded, I added, "Why won't you let yourself be saved?"

"It's not going to happen for me. I knew what I was doing when I planned this. I don't want you to get caught. If I stay with you, I'll hold you up. One person is harder to hunt than two. If I head back, I can lead him in the wrong direction."

"No, I won't let you go back," I said. "We're in this together. I'm not going to have that on my conscience. Besides, I have been alone in that dungeon for too long. Please don't leave me alone again."

He looked at me with sorrow in his eyes. "I've done enough to hurt you."

"So, make it up to me. Stay with me and get me out of these woods alive," I pleaded.

With a sigh and a nod, he picked up a roll and broke it in half before handing it to me.

22

It was dark, and I was cold. We hadn't talked for hours—just walked farther and farther into the woods. We weren't sure where we were going or if we were headed in the right direction. By the time the sun went down, I couldn't go any further.

"Can we stop just for a little while?" I looked at him with pleading eyes.

"I see a place to rest up ahead. Let's make it to the top of the hill where that covering is, and we'll stop there," he answered.

Using the spindly tree trunks to propel myself up the hill, we made it to the top. The covering seemed to be a tent that must have gotten carried away in the wind. The reaching branches of the large oak held it into place, making it the perfect place to rest.

I sat under the covering and pulled out the bottle of water. Shards of ice were crystalizing over the lid. I surrounded the lid with my hands in an attempt to coax it loose with my warm breath.

"Here, let me," he suggested as he took the water bottle before banging the tip against a sprawling root. With relief, he opened the lid and passed the water to me.

"You go," I said. "You haven't had much of anything."

He took a long pull on the bottle, taking in the icy water. Using his sleeve to wipe his mouth, he passed it to me. I took a drink, feeling its cold chill pour into my body. "This is going to make us freeze even more," I mentioned.

As we sat under the tree, waiting for morning, I leaned into him for warmth. Listening for every sound, I was alert to the wind rushing past my ears. In the distance, a squeal let out.

"What was that?!" I cried, sitting up.

"Probably some kind of big cat," he determined, "but he's more afraid of you than you are of it," he added.

I leaned back into his warm chest, covering my nose with my hands. Remembering the snowy ground I traveled during my last day at home, I was thankful to see that there was little to no snow left on the ground. Either we were farther away from home than I thought, or there had been some warmer days. Here, deep in the woods, I doubted the sun penetrated to the forest floor.

"Do you know where we are?" I asked out loud.

"Not really. When he takes me somewhere, he covers my face."

"Do you know where I live?" I asked, hoping he would be forthcoming with me.

"No, not really."

"But you know I live near the mall," I said matter-of-factly.

He looked at me before quickly looking away.

"I know who you are, Mason."

"How did you know? We barely spoke."

"I didn't, at first. I knew you looked familiar, but I didn't realize that you were the boy at the mall until later."

"I didn't want it to be you," he said quietly.

"You knew this would happen?" I asked, calmly, hoping he wouldn't clam up.

"That's why he took me there. He had a plan. While we were there, he overheard those kids saying they were meeting some girls. He made me start playing some games with them so he could set eyes on you and your friends. I'm sorry. I tried not to look at you. I knew if I looked at you, he would pick you."

"I remember. You held your head down and your hair was in your face. Anytime I looked at you, you looked away."

"It was hard not to look at you. I really didn't want him to take you, but I didn't know what to do. You saw my back – what he did to me. I wish I would have warned you."

"Did he tell you he chose me that day?"

"I knew," he said, pausing before adding, "After meeting you that day, and you and your friends went to the movie. He took me to the car, where he knocked me out. When I woke up, we were following you. He must have waited until the movie was over."

"How come you told the guys that he was your uncle?"

"That's what he told me to say."

"But he's your dad?"

"He says he's my dad. Always says no one else would ever want me."

"How old are you?"

"Fifteen. I think. I don't have birthdays, but I asked him once and he told me I was 14. That was probably about a year ago."

"Are you really homeschooled?" I questioned.

"Not really," he said, bringing his hand up to his face. Resting his chin in his hand, he added,

"That's what we tell everyone, but he's never taught me anything.

"Nothing? Not to read or do math or anything?"

"I can read, but he didn't teach me. I like reading, and he actually lets me read."

"If he never taught you how to read, how did you learn?"

"I'm not sure. I just don't remember ever not being able to read."

I looked at him inquisitively, wondering how it was possible for someone to teach themselves to read without toys or TV or even someone teaching them the alphabet.

"Do you remember living here forever?"

"For as long as I can remember."

"What's your earliest memory?" I questioned.

"I don't know. Maybe when I was six?"

I took a breath before speaking. "Mason. I don't think he's your dad. I think you might have been the boy my mom always warned me about."

"Huh? What do you mean?" he asked, turning his eyes toward me.

"When I was younger, my mom always said there was a boy that went missing when I was little. She was paranoid – well, at the time I thought she was paranoid; turns out she was right. But anyway, she was afraid of letting me go anywhere on my own."

"Nahh, it can't be me. I've been there as long as I can remember."

"But when something really bad happens, sometimes—"

"—Just stop. It's not me. I don't want to talk about it anymore."

A few minutes went by before I started in again with the questions. I had to know why this happened. I had to try and figure out who my captor was. If I ever made it back home, I was going to make him pay.

"What about the other girls?" I turned to look him in the eye.

"The other three?" he sighed. "I don't know what happened to them. He made me have sex with them on camera and soon strange men were coming in and having sex with them. All of the sudden, one day they were gone."

"Dead?"

"I don't think so. I saw some of the men give him money – way more than usual. I think they were buying the girls, rather than just buying time with the girls by that point."

With my eyes wide, I covered my mouth. Tears began welling up in my eyes. "That could've been me."

"That's why I wanted to get you out of there. I couldn't save the others, but I thought maybe I could save you." He reached out to my hands as I started to scoot away. "I didn't want this. I didn't ask for this, but I knew I could change it. I promise you... if I have to die trying, I will get you home."

23

"Mason...hey," I whispered, as the sun peeked through the trees.

"Hmm?" he said, sleepily.

"We fell asleep. I think we should go. We've been here too long."

"Crap!" He said, as he stirred himself awake. "It's probably just after dawn. He's probably not even awake yet."

"If he went back to the cabin," I finished.

"He's a lazy son-of-a-bitch. There's no way he stayed out here in the cold."

"Let's head this way," as he took the bags from my arms.

We continued in the direction Mason suggested, listening for cars on the road or running water. We didn't talk, reserving our energy for the trek that lay ahead.

Mason reached into the bag and pulled out some raisins, "I know it's not much, but you need to eat something," he said.

"What I need is a fire," I said in response, getting crabbier by the minute.

"I considered building one last night, but I think the wood is too wet. Plus, I didn't want to attract attention."

We continued through the woods, stopping every few minutes to catch our breath. We planned to ration the water, but our thirst won out. Mason held the last of the water out to me and said, "You need to drink this. Maybe we'll find a stream and can get some more water later, but you haven't had anything to drink since last night."

I obliged and took the last swig in the bottle, savoring every last drop. Chucking the bottle back into the satchel, I pulled the blanket out, wrapping it around my shoulders.

We continued to walk until my leg buckled beneath me and I fell to my knees. With his hand grasping my elbow, he pulled me up, eyeing me with concern.

"Is it your leg?"

"I think so," I said, wincing in pain. The bullet just grazed me, but it never really healed. It might be infected." I added.

He walked me to a tree, where he leaned me against its rough trunk. With his back to me, he looked out into the forest. Taking about ten paces into the thick trees, he bent over and returned to me, carrying a large, sturdy stick. Handing it to me with one hand, he used the other to help steady me.

"I don't know if I can make it," I whined. "I think I'm just done. People don't live in the freezing cold for a reason. Most people would have died out here last night."

"I know. That's why we aren't going to give up."

"But I can't! I just can't! I sobbed. "After everything that's happened, would dying be so bad?"

"Shhh!" he said as he raised a finger to his lips.

"Don't shush me!" I yelled. "I have every right—"

With that, he put his hand over my mouth and cupped his ear, straining to hear.

24

My eyes widened and my mouth formed the shape of an "O." Collecting our stuff, we rushed down the hill, toward the sounds of a car rushing by.

"Stop!" I yelled, hoping the driver would see us in his rear view mirror and pick us up. With tears in my eyes, the defeat hit me hard.

Mason looked backward, expecting to see more cars. There were none. "It won't be long. Surely someone else will come down this road."

"This is like a little country road," I said in frustration. "It's not like a zillion people are going to pass by."

"But someone has to live down this way," he reasoned.

Just then, another car flew by, ignoring us. We looked at each other, with defeat in my eyes, yet hope in his.

We kept walking. It was at least thirty minutes before another car came by. As we waved them down, the carful of teens slowed just long enough to throw a beer can out the window at us, roaring in laughter as the car sped off.

We came upon an overpass, opting to scale down the hillside to the stream below. Fearful we'd miss another car, I wanted to be quick, but

I was so thirsty. I cupped my hands and dunked them into the cool water. Pulling them to my lips, I drew in the water.

As I waited for Mason to finish filling the bottle with water, I leaned back on the bank. He came to sit beside me and put his hand over mine.

I looked over at him. "I have something to say that you're not going to like, but hear me out," he started. "I want to get you home, too, but I think we should stop for the night." As I opened my mouth in protest, he raised his eyebrows and held his hands up to stop me. "It's going to get dark soon and if we stay under this overpass, we'll be out of the wind, we'll have water, and we can keep checking to see if anyone is coming. When it gets darker, the air is going to get colder again. I really don't know if we'll make it out here another night, but we certainly won't if we are out in the wind. At least in the woods, there were barriers from the wind."

"Ok, but if I hear any cars coming, I'm going up," I answered as we made our way under the overpass. We found a built up area of dirt from the last time the creek was high and snuggled together for warmth under the blanket.

"Mason...thanks," I said, as I closed my eyes.

"You're welcome," he answered, adding, "Thank you, Josie."

"For what?" I inquired.

"You saved my life," he responded. Noticing my confusion, he added, "If my life ends tonight, you've made me a better person. This is the way I'd want it to end."

Before hearing everything he said, I was asleep.

25

I awoke in a panic, rising from the cold, damp ground. My breathing was heavy and erratic as I searched for a way to protect myself.

"Josie – It's okay. You're safe now."

As I realized that the dream was my recent reality, I cried, "No! No, I'm not. I'll never be the same. He's taken everything from me. I'm no longer whole. I'm going to live the rest of my life fixated on what has happened. He's taken my body, but what's worse is that he's stolen my mind! I have no thoughts of my own anymore – they consist of darkness and cruelty." I wrapped my arms around myself, sobbing. I jerked from his touch as he laid his hand on my shoulder. "Don't touch me."

Pulling back, he said, "I'm sorry. I know I've hurt you. I know you have no reason to forgive me. I thought that – well, last night, you seemed like you were more comfortable with me. It's stupid of me to think you could ever see me as a friend. I will get you home and you'll never have to see me again. I'd understand."

I stood and walked from him. With my back to him, I held myself against the cold, blowing breeze. I knew that wasn't what I wanted. As much as I wished I had never met him, I also knew he was trying to save me. Under different circumstances, we could have been friends. He was willing to give himself up to save me. My tears dried against my face as I breathed deep to calm my thumping heart. Several moments passed before I spoke.

"I don't want that. I just need some time. I know you were hurt by him. Even though you aren't convinced, you aren't his kid, and whatever he did to you screwed you up just like it's doing to me. I want to forgive you, and believe it or not, I want to protect you from him. But right now, I'm panicked. I can't sleep without seeing him. I can't walk without feeling the bullet that grazed my leg. My wrists are oozing with puss – a reminder of being imprisoned. And not only that, but my privacy and my innocence were ripped from me. I was robbed of my childhood.

I'm 13 and I will never be a normal teenager, even if I do make it out alive."

I continued to stand with my back facing him. Thinking about the words I just spoke, I almost felt guilty for putting that burden on him.

"Your life is ruined," he said. "I know that – and I know that I had a part in it. I'm taking that responsibility, and I'll get you to your family. It's going to suck. We're going to scream, cry, yell, fight, and the dreams will keep haunting us. But I will be here through it all."

A moment passed in silence before I asked, "Did you ever have dreams like that?"

"All the time."

"When did they start?"

"For as long as I can remember. You can't be in a cage and not have nightmares about it. You can't have happy dreams when you are whipped. But I always prayed for it to stop. The day I got you out, I knew that God was giving me the courage to do what I could never do before.

"How do you know about God? Surely your dad isn't someone who goes to church."

"I don't know. You hear stuff, you know."

"No. I don't think that's it," I said, as I turned to him. "You know about God because you had a life before this."

As I spoke, he shook his head and let his long hair fall over his face as he looked at the ground.

"Seriously, listen to me," I said, as I knelt beside him. "You are remembering things, but you don't know what you are remembering them from. There's a past there. Please, try and remember."

He was silent for a few moments before I interrupted his thinking. "What's your middle name?"

"Jason," he said, without missing a beat.

"He named you Mason Jason?" I inquired, proving my point that he had a previous life. "I think your name before was Jason. It was the first name that came to your mind just now."

"I feel kinda sick," he said, trying to change the subject. "Can we just sit here quietly until the sun comes up? We don't have much time before we have to start moving again."

"Yeah."

Ten minutes went by without a word. I tried to recall the name of the little boy that went missing. The name Michael kept entering my mind, but that was nothing close to Jason. I closed my eyes, trying to remember the story Mom told me. *Was he five or six when he was taken? It was just one town over, Mom said. Would a kidnapper keep him here, this close to where he lived? ...Michael? Mitchell?* It was driving me crazy.

The roar of a truck went by. Mason looked at me and jumped up. Gripping the dried grass on the embankment, he clawed his way up to the street.

"No!" I screamed. "He took me in a truck. It could be him!"

"I'll stay low. I just want to see who's coming," he yelled over the truck's engine.

The sun had already started to peek over the horizon as he spied the road from behind the guardrail. His clothes were dirty and torn. He had let me use the blanket almost the entire time we were out here. I wondered about his feet, looking at their blue hue, I realized that he hadn't had shoes this entire time. I took them off and left them next to him as I began gathering our belongings.

"It's a school bus!" he jumped out from behind the guardrail. The bus swerved and honked as it flew by.

"Shit! Shit! Shit! Why won't anyone stop?" he complained.

"...Because they don't expect to see a dirty, ragged teenager approaching them as they drive by at the crack of dawn."

I climbed up the hill toward him. "Hey, put those on," I said pointing at the shoes. "I've had them long enough. " Your feet are blue."

As he slid the shoes over his feet, he winced, signaling signs of possible frostbite.

"You okay to start walking?" I asked.

"Yeah, I just need to go slow."

After thirty minutes of walking, we found a cross street.

"Which way?" I asked out loud.

"I don't think it matters."

Rather than play a game of Eeny Meeny Miney Moe, I decided to go left. It seemed like it would be the farthest from my kidnapper's cabin, although I was so turned around it could have led us straight to his door.

"I wish we had found a busier road," I mentioned.

"Out here, there are no busy roads. That's why he keeps this place. He is secretive and keeps to himself... thinks people are out to get him."

"They probably are... if they know anything about him."

"True."

We walked in silence for another hour or so, wondering if we would ever find civilization, when all of the sudden a car began approaching from behind. I turned to look and saw a small, dark car pulling up slowly behind us.

"You two okay?" the driver asked.

I hurried toward the door to beg for help when Mason's arm gripped mine.

"Don't. You Need To Run—Now!"

26

"Mason, what are you talking about? This is our chance!" I reasoned.

"Josie, don't."

As I got closer, I could see the driver. A familiarity overtook my senses. *Could it really be him? He's the one to rescue me? It's been so long...would I even recognize him?*

"Mason, I think it's my dad!" I said, as I looked at him cheerfully. I headed toward the car as I heard the door open.

"No, Josie, it's not your dad. I know him. Please, come with me, NOW!"

"No, Mason—it's him!" I said. I turned my back to the car and walked backwards trying to coax Mason to accompany me.

"Josie, is that you?" I heard from a distance.

I turned to see him. He didn't look like I remembered. He was bigger, but I was sure it was him. He knew my name, after all.

I headed toward him, smiling. As I approached, I said, "Come on, Mason—get in!"

Before I could finish, I felt a gloved hand wrap around my mouth. I tried to call out, asking him why he was doing this to me, but I still didn't understand what was happening. As he dragged me to the car, I tried to struggle. He pointed a gun at Mason and said, "You, too, get in the car."

Mason looked as though he were struggling to decide whether to get in the car or make a run for it. His conflicted eyes moved between me and the gun.

I was shoved in the back seat before the door was shut, where I sat banging on the window, screaming in confusion.

Mason made his way to the car, eyeing the pistol before him.

As he got in, he said, "This isn't your dad, Josie. This guy is one of the guys who comes and gets money from my dad. He's the one who set up the appointments for all those men that came in and hurt you."

"Shut up or I'll put a fucking bullet in your brain," the voice from the front seat commanded. "Let me think. I need to think."

Mason looked at me and mouthed, *It's true.*

I looked at Mason with sorrow in my eyes, not knowing what to believe. I hadn't seen my dad in so many years that maybe I just wanted it to be him. I wanted him to save me. It looked like him...it had to be him. But why would he be doing this?

"Is it true?" I asked. "Are you the guy that he's seen?"

"I said shut the fuck up!" he said, as he tapped the barrel of the pistol against his head, "think...think...think."

"But you're my dad. I recognize you – from my memory and from pictures."

"I'm nobody's dad," he said calmly, as he put the gun on the passenger seat and lit a cigarette.

Mason, holding the satchel, gave a sideways glance. I put my hand on the satchel between us to be near him. I quietly opened the pocket, retrieving the sharpened stone I had worked on in my cell, glad I stashed it for safekeeping. I opened his fingers and placed the stone into his palm, rewrapping his fingers around it. Mason nodded to show his understanding as I distracted the driver with questions.

"That's not true. I know it's you. Besides, how did you know my name?"

"Look. I don't know you. I don't care about you. I never wanted you. I don't have any kids."

Even now, at this moment, with a crazy man driving me to my doom, I felt kicked in the gut. I knew it was him. Tears began to emerge when I realized what I'd have to do. I knew I should feel nothing for the sack of shit that was never around. I needed to save Em from a life of wishing for her dad to come home.

As I waited to make my move, I said, "Why did you do this?"

"It's all about the money. I got no feelings toward you. I don't know you. I don't want to know you. No one never gave me nothin'. I gotta get what I need, and this is the fastest way to do it," he said matter-of-factly.

"He's the one who sets up the appointments. He gets the money when guys come and make a payment to—" Before Mason could finish, he cut him off while waving the gun around, pointing it toward the back seat.

"—I told you to shut your fucking mouth. If Eric woulda just got me my money, none of this ever would have happened. I told that fucker he owed me and he'd better pay up!"

What? I thought. *Eric is involved?* Rather than asking more questions, I just waited in hopes that he would say more.

"I told Eric he could have that bitch – your mom—by keep'n me happy. Gots to keep me happy to keep 'er. He didn't do that. He didn't bring me money. So I took somethin' of his.

You's gonna earn me my money. I got a business to run."

Mason had hidden the stone underneath his right leg, waiting for the right moment. We sat in silence for what seemed like forever, but it probably only lasted a few minutes.

Up ahead, I saw a small gas station. Looking at Mason, I tipped my head forward, hoping he would look up and see it. He looked at me and mouthed, *Ready?* I nodded, holding my breath. As we approached the stop sign nearing the gas station, I put my hand on the door handle, ready to spring into action.

When the car slowed to a stop, Mason whipped up his arm, stabbing the stone into the driver's eye.

"GO!" Mason yelled.

I pulled on the handle, struggling to free myself. As I fumbled with the lock, trying to get out of the moving prison, I cried out, "I can't!"

Mason leaned over the front seat, reaching for the gun. Bringing it back and knocking it against the window, he cleared the way. As I struggled to dive through the window, the car started accelerating. Flopping out of the car and rolling to freedom with my face and shoulder bloodied, I jumped up and ran towards the gas station. I looked back, hoping to see Mason following. All I saw was the car driving erratically.

I turned back and headed inside. As the bells rang over the door, I looked at the gas station attendant, fell to my knees, and said, "Help me!"

He came out from behind the counter and offered to help me to my feet, but I shuffled backward to conceal my body between the aisles. "What's your name, sweetheart?" the older man asked gently.

"Josie. And there's a boy in the car out there, too. Please help us! I've been kidnapped!"

As he rounded the counter, he picked up the phone. While dialing 911, he looked out the window. Picking up a rifle, he headed for the door. I peeked around a display at the end of the aisle and saw Mason running toward the door. I grabbed the attendant's leg and said,

"No!"

"He's got a gun!" the attendant said.

"It's not his! He stole it from the car! Don't shoot!"

He tentatively lowered the rifle, eyeing Mason as he ran toward the door.

"Put the gun down, son," he said, as Mason slammed through the door.

His head was bleeding; streams of blood were flowing down from the sticky wound beneath his hair. He set the gun down and fell to the ground, his face landing on my lap. As his hair fell to the side, I saw a branch sticking out from his neck. I looked up at the attendant who was hanging up with the police. My heart stopped as I choked back the tears. I began to pull on the branch, when the attendant stopped me.

"Don't. Leave it for the doctors. He could bleed out." Noting my confusion, he elaborated, saying, "The stick is better where it is right now. It's holding pressure on the wound. He might die if you take it out."

I nodded and sat there, waiting, tears breeching the edge of my lids, exhausted.

"I'm Bill," he said, as he handed me a water bottle. "I'm going to be here by your side until the police get here. We're going to close down until that happens. You don't have to see anyone or talk to anyone until they get here. But if you want anything, you can talk to me."

"Thanks," I said, taking the water. "Can I have…"

"—anything. Whatever you want. It's yours."

"A Twinkie?"

"You got it," he said with a smile.

He locked up the doors and went to retrieve the Twinkies.

As I held the Twinkie, poised to unwrap it, I looked at my hands. They were filthy. My fingernails were caked with dirt, blood mapping over my hands, and gravel imbedded into my skin. I started crying. I took the bottle of water and poured it over my hands, watching the dirt and blood flow off, frantically trying to rid myself of the last several days or weeks or however long I had been away.

Moments later, I heard the sirens as they approached the station. Bill unlocked the door and let the police officers inside. They looked from me to a paper, nodding to one another before one finally said, "Are you Josie Fogel?"

I nodded.

"We've got you. You're safe."

I sighed, the tears still streaming down my face as an EMT placed a blanket around my shoulders.

"Can you walk?" she asked.

I stood, my knees buckling, but determined to stay upright, I held on to her. She looked at my wrists, noticing the restraint marks. "I am going to need to put you on a gurney, but I won't strap you in. Is that okay?" she asked gently.

Again, I nodded.

Soon dozens of agents entered the gas station. A woman came in and stayed with me while they put me in the ambulance. "My name is Officer Lots, but you can call me Mary. Would it be okay if I take some pictures of you and get some samples from your skin, clothes, fingernails, and hair when we get to the hospital?"

"Yes, but I poured water on them," I said, as I held my hands up to show her.

"That's okay. We'll work with what we have."

"Are you taking Mason to the same hospital?" I asked, concern flooding my voice.

"We'll make sure he's taken care of," she said.

As the ambulance drove away, I heard the driver call back to the EMT who was checking me out. "I remember when a boy was taken around here. It was the year I had my Ashley. Scared the dickens out of me. I think that was him – Jason Carmichael."

Carmichael! I recalled. No wonder I was thinking the boy's name was Michael.

27

Twenty minutes later, we were at the hospital. The police chief and several officers meandered around my room while the nurses washed and wrapped my wounds behind the curtain.

"What happened to Mason?"

The nurse looked at me with sadness in her eyes. "You mean the boy you were with? He's in surgery. The branch penetrated his neck. It didn't hit anything major, but they want to remove it carefully so it doesn't nick a nearby artery. He will be okay, but he's very malnourished. He's been gone a long time. He hasn't eaten well. It's going to take a long time to get him back to good health. But we're taking good care of him."

Officer Lots came in, and after snapping her photos, she took my hand in hers and began taking samples from beneath my nails. A detective moved the curtain aside asking if he could ask me some questions.

I looked up and said, "Yes."

"I know there's a lot to remember, but we'll focus on the most important information for now. We'll let you get some rest, and we can pick back up on the less pertinent details later. Is that okay?"

"Yes, I think that would be fine."

"First, your family is on their way. They know you are here. We called them right away. We're about 45 minutes from your hometown, so it's going to be a little bit, but they will be here. Now, I want to start with where you were kept. Can you tell me a little bit about it?"

"It was a cabin in the woods. I'm not sure where. He kept me in a room in the basement. It was locked all the time. I couldn't see anything."

"Did you notice anything when you got away?"

"No, just trees. I didn't even know if we were going the right way."

"That's okay. Is there anything you can remember about your abductor?"

"Not really. Most of the time it was dark. I only remember a little bit from when he took me. He had dark hair – about my color."

He nodded as he took notes, being careful not to push too fast.

"And he was probably about your height." I added, "and maybe like 30 years old?"

"And the man in the car, what was that about?"

Tears flooded my eyelids as I recalled the hurtful, angry man I once knew as my dad.

"It was… He tried to take us back! We had to get out. It wasn't our fault!" I rambled, not making sense. The officer placed his hand over mine and looked at me in the eyes. "It's ok. You got out alive. You did what you had to do. But, you seemed to know who he was. You were mumbling to the gas station attendant. Did you know him, Josie?"

I couldn't speak. I just looked at the officer while trying to slow my breathing as he continued to talk.

"His car was wrapped around a tree. But he's not in it. We are canvassing the area. The car is registered to a Chuck Butler. Do you know him?"

"No, that's not Chuck Butler," I managed to say.

I didn't elaborate, finding it difficult to find the words to tell him who my latest captor really was.

"So you knew him? Had you seen him before?"

I looked down before saying, "It was Jim Fogel."

"James Fogel, your dad?" he questioned.

"Yes. He said he didn't want anything to do with me and that he doesn't have kids. He had a crazy look in his eyes."

A few minutes went by before I looked at him and added, "He was behind all this. Ask Mason. He was the one who had me and the other girls abducted. He had the men come in and—and—" I couldn't finish as I shook; my sobs overtaking my entire body.

The questioning went on like this for thirty minutes when I heard my mom's voice.

"Where is she?" she said frantically.

"Whelp," the detective said, "It sounds like your mom and step-dad are here."

Before leaving, he leaned down and said, "I'm Detective Falcor. You be sure to call me with anything else you remember. I'm going to let you rest and we'll talk again soon, okay?" He smiled at me, as my mom and Eric swept the curtain aside and enveloped me in their arms.

"Josie, thank God!" my mom exclaimed. "I thought we'd lost you!"

Tears were streaming down her face as she held my face in both hands, looking me over as if she hadn't seen me before, taking in all my features.

The tears flowed freely as I looked at my mom and Eric, begging them to hold me and never let me go.

I'd never seen Eric cry before. He looked at me and smiled, with tears in his eyes, saying, "Josie. I love you, I love your mom, and I love Em. You all are everything to me. I should have told you that before. I was afraid I would never get the chance to tell you that again, kid."

I smiled at him, wanting to tell him that I love him, too, but having so many questions. I was tired. I just wanted to go home and see Em. I didn't want to talk any more.

The doctor entered. "Doctor, when will she be released?" my mom asked.

"Ma'am, she's been through a lot. She's severely dehydrated. She's only 77 pounds. Her blood levels are off, her blood pressure is high, her heart rate is low. We have a lot of work here to do."

"I understand that, Doctor, and I don't want to rush her either, but I am afraid to have her stay here."

"Excuse me—" Detective Falcor peeked through the curtain. "I'm sorry to interrupt, but I want to assure you that once the nurses are done processing her, the doctors will move her to a private room and we will keep two officers outside her room at all times."

Angie looked at Detective Falcor and nodded her approval.

Just then, we heard sobs crying, "Where is he? It's been so long. Where *is* he?! I know it has to be my Jason! Please, let me see him," she moaned.

I looked at my mom and tears began to well up in my eyes. "He saved my life," I said.

***

By nightfall, I was in my own room. I didn't watch TV because my face was plastered on the screen everywhere. It was too intense.

I didn't have much to eat. Although I wanted food, I was unable to keep the Twinkie down from earlier. The doctors said it was because my body didn't know how to react after being starved for six weeks.

Six weeks, I thought to myself. I knew it had been a while. The nurses suggested I start out with something very bland and small. They kept an IV of saline in me to provide nutrients. Once I could keep food down, I would be allowed to go home.

I hadn't said much to my parents about the ordeal yet. I wasn't sure I wanted to get into the details. I wanted to ask Eric what he knew about my abduction, but I didn't know how, especially in front of my mom.

"Mom, can you go ask the doctors about Mason? And see if you can find his mom and tell her that he saved my life."

"Absolutely, honey. I will be right back." She stopped stroking my arm with her fingernails, something she did whenever I was sick, and set the magazine down on my bed.

When the door closed, I looked at Eric and said, "It was my dad. He's the one who set all this up."

Eric looked at the floor and brought his hand up to his face, stroking his stubble.

For I think what could have been the first time ever, he looked up and into my eyes. "I let you down, Josie. I knew your dad was bad news. I got into some trouble with him years back. He was a sick man. I knew he had his demons. When he left, I wanted to take care of you and Em and your mom. I loved you—I mean, I love you—all three of you. You're my family," he corrected.

"He said you owed him money and if you had paid him..." I trailed.

"When he showed up a few months ago, he said he wanted money. I didn't have it to give. I never thought he would be a part of something so awful, Jos. I didn't have the extra money; I had given him all I had already. And every time he would show up at work, I would lose hours and that would eat into the paycheck. I had to start taking out loans just to pay the bills. I would never put you at risk like that. You know that, right, kid?"

The way he called me kid used to bug me, but today it felt endearing. I smiled and shook my head.

"I know I have a lot of work to do." He continued, "I have a lot of making up ahead of me. I know it won't be easy and I know I haven't been the best step-dad. It was new to me, you know—being a dad—taking on that role."

I looked down and picked at my fingernails as he spoke until I felt his finger on my chin. As he guided my gaze to his, he spoke, "I love you. I love our family. You are not my step-daughter, you are my daughter. Don't ever forget that. Don't ever doubt that. I'm going to take the rest of my life being your dad and making up for my shortcomings. I'm going to make mistakes. But I will never stop loving you. What you've been through is unimaginable. I hate myself for not being there to protect you. And right now, things seem good. But they are surreal. This is the beginning of the healing—the healing for all of us. It's going to take a lot of work, a lot of patience, and a lot of therapy. We'll get there. But for now, you need to rest. Just know that I'm never leaving your side."

I couldn't find the words to express how I was feeling. I was overwhelmed with emotion. This was a man who had not said much to me since becoming my step-dad. I always knew he worked hard for us and tried to give us the things we needed and wanted, but what I didn't know was that he was fighting his own battle behind the scenes all this time.

I smiled a weak smile through the tears and squeezed his hand.

Moments later, Mom came through the door and was at my side. "I can't believe I left you in here that long. I lose you for six weeks and I don't want to be gone one minute longer! But, I did find out that the boy you were with is out of surgery. He will be here for several more days before they'll release him."

"Can I see him before I leave?" I interjected.

"Um, sure, I guess so," Mom said, looking taken aback.

Wanting to explain myself, I said, "Mom, if he weren't there, I don't know if I would have lived long enough to escape. Then, when we did escape, he made sure I made it home alive."

"I understand, sweetie. I'm just worried about you."

"I know, Mom. I know."

28

Being missing for six weeks, I would have thought that the next few days in the hospital would have been a breeze. The stares, the questions, the poking and prodding were all more than I could take. Last night was the worst. I woke up from a nightmare and landed in my nightmare of reality. The truth is, I just wanted to be at home, in my room, and to stop talking about the kidnapping.

Bathed in sweat, I lifted the weighted covers off my body and rose from the bed. The cool air hit the sweat covering my body, causing a shiver to run down my spine.

I quietly left the room, making sure not to wake Mom.

I pulled the door open and exited into the hallway, quietly spotting an officer slumped over in his chair. His coffee, cresting the lid of his cup, threated to spill over. I held the door as I allowed it to close quietly behind me while holding my breath. Tired of the freedom I once had being kept at bay, I was done being held captive. Six weeks was enough. The simple act of walking the hallway and getting my own blanket strengthened my resolve to be free. I slowly crept along the wall, hoping to stay inconspicuous while on the hunt for a clean, dry blanket. I approached a room that read *Linens* and peered through the crack in the door.

"Missy, aren't you supposed to be in bed?" I hear from behind. I twirled around, my heart caught in my throat. Startled, I backed into the door, causing the door to close with a bang.

"Did that Officer Ludwig fall asleep? He is supposed to tell me if he leaves your door, you know." The African American woman clicked away, typing on the keyboard as she smacked her gum. When I didn't answer, she looked up with big brown eyes surrounded by long, lush lashes. She offered a comforting smile. "Honey, what's the matter?"

"I was hot. I mean cold." I cringed, knowing I wasn't making any sense. "I woke up sweating and my blankets are soaking wet."

"Oh, sure sweetie! Let's get you some fresh linens. Do you need a new gown?"

"That might be nice." I smiled politely.

As she spun in the chair, a nurse approached behind her and teasingly said, "Adelaide, are you playing on my computer again?" The middle-aged, heavy-set woman sauntered around the desk.

"Yes, Nurse Mary. I'm sorry. I was sending an email to Rowan."

"I told you not to call me that, Adelaide—plain old Mary is just fine. As I said before, you can use the computer. I know you look forward to talking to your son. How is he doing at the base?"

"Oh, I miss him somethin' terrible. But he's doing good. Should be able to come back for Christmas."

"That's wonderful! So, who do we have here, Adelaide?" she asked, noticing my presence.

"Oh, Nurse Mary—I mean, Mary, this is Josie. She's not sleeping well tonight. I'm about to get her some fresh linens. But would you take a look at her bandages? They look like they need changing."

I looked down toward my wrists and saw the green hue beneath them.

"Oh, Josie, you're—"

"Yep, I'm the one," hoping to finish her thought so we didn't have to talk about it.

"Yes, Room 121. I just started my shift, so I haven't gone over intake reports yet. I've been in Florida for a week."

Crap. I don't want to explain, I thought. "I'll just wait for the blankets in my room," I said quickly as I scurried down the hallway.

Officer Ludwig was still slumped over in his chair by the time I reached my door. I pushed it open and felt resistance on the other side.

29

I didn't have time to react before Mom swung the door open. "Josie, did he do anything to you? Where is he? Where did he go?"

"Mom, I'm okay! You're dreaming. I'm fine. I'm here. I just needed a new blanket."

"No, he was here!" she insisted, as she kicked the officer's foot. "What were you doing—sleeping??? A man was here. In Josie's room!"

"That's impossible ma'am. We have officers at all the entrances."

"He was standing right in front of me. He had a gun for God's sake!"

The officer pulled out his radio and held it to his face. "Rigsby, what's your 20?" After no response, he tried another officer. "Carter, what's your 20?"

"I'm still here. West wing, elevators, Lud."

"Have you heard from Rigsby?"

"Nope. I'll go have a look."

"Mrs. McIntosh, what did the man say? What did he look like?"

"He said to shut our mouths. He said, 'I'll get that B if she gives me up.' He had a gun. He put it to my head!" she exclaimed, as she touched just above her ear.

Just then, the radio crackled. "Officer down! I have an officer down at the east wing stairwell between the first and second floors of Grace Memorial. Send backup and paramedics—now!"

"Carter, what you got?" Ludwig questioned.

"Rigsby's down. Been sh—shot."

Frozen in fear, I stood silent.

"I need you both to get in your room and block the door with whatever you can find," Officer Ludwig said before shouting to a nearby nurse, "Get on the intercom. Lock this place down. No one inside or out. Got it?"

Her eyes widened as she shook her head. She picked up a nearby phone on the wall and spoke calmly, "put lock-down procedures in place. No one in or out. Be on the lookout for a—

" she paused, waiting for the officer to fill in the blank.

Trotting down the hallway, he called back, "—a man with a gun. That's all I know. I have to help my officer. Find a safe place to hide!"

30

Mom and I backed into the darkened room.

"You okay, Mom?"

"Me? Honey, don't worry about me. You've been through so much. Here. Help me move this cabinet."

With all our efforts, the cabinet wasn't moving. "Those chairs aren't going to hold anything closed. They'll just slide if someone tries to push the door open. Let's try the bed."

"It's got wheels."

"Shit!" Mom said as she walked into the bathroom. Leaning against the door, I let my head fall back onto the door and closed my eyes. *God, please protect us.* My prayer was interrupted by the sound of banging.

I opened my eyes. "Mom?"

She emerged with a towel bar and fit one side of the bar through the door handle, fitting the other end behind the cabinet to brace it in place.

We backed up and sat on the bed, our eyes locked on the door. Mom grabbed my hand and placed it in hers.

"Who—"

"I don't know, sweetie. I was asleep and it was dark."

***

It seemed like we were confined to that room forever. The door moved as someone tried to open it. As it rattled, mom strengthened her grip on my hand.

"It's Officer Ludwig; you can open the door."

Mom approached the door with caution. Sliding the bar out, she held it up, ready to strike as the door opened. As he stepped through the room, Mom said, "Well? Where is he?" as she put the towel bar down.

"He made it out before the hospital went on lockdown."

"What?! He's gone. Again? Detective Falcor said he would have this place covered! What were you thinking? You risked my daughter's life!"

Officer Ludwig fell silent. With his head hung low, he let out a breath. "Mrs. McIntosh, I don't know what to say."

"You can start by telling me what you are going to do."

"We've got people on it. An officer was killed, but they got some information from him before he passed."

I gasped.

"He was shot in the back."

Mom held her arms up. "And no one noticed? No one heard a shot?!"

He placed his left hand on his hip and his right rested on his gun, and he took a breath before he spoke. "I don't know, Mrs. McIntosh. He could have used a silencer. And, that stairwell is adjacent to the cafeteria. Hospital staff were prepping for morning orders, so there was a lot of commotion that could have masked the sound."

"What did the officer who was killed say?" I wondered out loud.

"He didn't see much. He'd stepped into the stairwell to make a phone call and heard a noise behind the door. He said he pulled his gun and began to turn when the shot was fired. He landed at the bottom of the stairs and was out cold until Officer Carter got to him. All he knew was that it was a white man, probably about 220 pounds." Looking at Mom, Officer Ludwig took his hat off and ran his fingers through this hair before saying, "Detectives will be here soon to get your statement. Do you think you can remember anything?"

"I didn't see anything. It was dark. I was asleep and woke up to his foul breath and hissing voice. I barely looked at him, but yes, he was white. Maybe mid-to-late thirties," she guessed. "He was worried about Josie giving him up. He just kept saying that she can't give him up. He's got a business to run, and she better not get in the way or he'll kill me, Eric, Emily, and Josie. He *knew* who we are! He mentioned Emily and Eric by name, too. He said he's been watching us."

31

I could hear officers in the hallway. Just then, a female detective knocked on the open door and introduced herself as Detective Silba and her partner as Detective Wright. Behind them were a man and woman wearing black jumpsuits with latex gloves and coverings over their feet.

"These are crime scene techs. We've got some techs in the stairwell, but we wanted to bring these two in here to see if they find anything. Will you two come with us to the waiting room down the hallway?"

"Mom grabbed her purse, and we followed the detectives down the hall to a room on the left. Detective Silba closed the door behind us and pointed to my wrists. "You need new bandages."

"Oh, yeah. The nurse was going to take care of that before—well, you know."

"We'll get her back here in a moment. Josie, you spoke to Detective Falcor when you arrived, but you were having trouble describing your abductor. Have you remembered anything else since then?"

I looked down, ashamed. "Not really. I mean, I can picture him, but I'm having trouble with details. Detective Falcor was going to have a sketch artist come up, but I haven't met him yet.

Most of my time was in the dark. When he would

open the door, my eyes couldn't adjust to the

light. I never really saw him for long."

"Ok, what about when he took you. Was

there anything that stood out?"

"Not really."

While pacing the room, Mom spoke up.

"What about the cabin where she was held? Have

they found it?"

"The cabin was burned to the ground.

There's nothing left in the house to process.

Officers are covering the grounds around the

cabin, though."

"But what about property records?"

"The cabin was owned by a man named

Chuck Butler, a former metal worker who would

be about retirement age. The car that Jim Fogel was driving was Chuck Butler's as well. We've got officers looking for Mr. Butler, but by all appearances, he is missing."

Biting my nails, I looked at Detective Silba and asked, "Do you think he's dead?"

"We won't know that until we finish our investigation. He could have been killed. He could have been a part of the criminal network. We don't really know."

"Excuse me, Detectives," Adelaide interrupted, after a quick knock on the door. "Miss Josie, here's your blanket. The technicians are finished with your room, so you can return there when you are finished here. Nurse Mary will be in to change your bandages. And breakfast will be served soon. Okay, sugar?"

As Adelaide turned to leave I blurted out, "Can't I just go home? I'm ready to go home." The tears were too strong to fight off.

"Honey, the nurse will talk to the doctors, and they'll have to clear you for discharge. I'll see if I can find out what their plans are for you." With that, she turned and walked out of the room.

"Detective." My mom pulled out a letter and passed it to Detective Silba before continuing. "What's the best way to get this out to the public? It's a letter thanking the public, but asking for our privacy. Eric is at home taking care of things around the house and caring for Em. He said there are news media and people driving past the house. How is Josie going to heal with all this going on?"

"We've been conferring with our psychologist. It is his recommendation that we place you in a safe house for the time being where you can all have some time to heal from this. Let the news story die down a bit before you head home. In fact, Dr. Mertz will want to meet with Josie."

"Ok, just tell us what we need to do."

32

Detectives Silba and Wright left, and I looked at my mom. "Do we have to go somewhere else? The only place I want to be is at home!"

"It's the best thing right now, Josie. We know what these guys are capable of. Not to mention, Jim knows where we live. I'm sorry, baby. It's what needs to be done."

We walked down the hallway toward my room, my eyes darted left and right, waiting for the other shoe to drop.

Nurse Mary was in my room when we arrived. "When can I leave?" I asked immediately upon entering.

Without answering my question she said, "Dr. Mertz is coming in at 9 o'clock. As she spoke, she unwrapped my bandage and cleaned out the wounds. I hadn't had IV antibiotics since the day I arrived, so I didn't really understand what I was still doing there.

Placing the new gauze over the wound, I winced. "Sorry, dear. I know it's still sore. You have quite an infection in there. The culture came back and we're going to have to put you on another round of IV antibiotics."

"So, how long?"

She unwrapped a plastic covering and placed it over a thermometer. "Open."

I opened my mouth as she stuck the thermometer in and closed it back again.

"Once we get the fever down, we'll know the infection is on its way out. Hopefully then, you'll be released."

The thermometer beeped. "102.2 degree temp. You need to get back in bed. I'll start a line in a few minutes."

Mom turned the television on as I settled in bed. The 8 o'clock news came on. *Had we been awake for that many hours already?*

Gracing the screen was a Paris Hilton look-alike anchor standing in front of burning remains.

I sat up. "Mom—That's it. That's where I was." I stared in awe.

"I'll turn it off."

As mom rose to flip the switch, I put my hand up. "No, wait. I want to know what's happening."

She turned the volume up. The anchor was in mid-sentence. "—held captive here. The kidnapper appears to have left in a hurry, leaving behind a car and although the shed out back was doused with gasoline, it was never lit. Forensic detectives are combing through the rubble hoping to find clues. The owner of the cabin, Chuck Butler, is a 71-year-old retiree. He was never married, nor did he have children. His involvement is unknown. This is Darcy McKnight, reporting—"

"Darcy," another news anchor broke in. "We are having reports of some activity in the back. Can you tell us what you see?"

With the shaky camera following behind, the anchor walked farther into the scene, looking backward, toward the cameraman every few seconds as she spoke. "The detectives are being very tight-lipped about their findings, but it does appear that they have found something. They are suiting up in yellow jumpsuits and one is carrying a shovel. They appear to be dismantling the pile of firewood in the back. I can't tell if they found something, but," she broke connection with the camera and looked behind to the cameraman.

"Ian, can you zoom in on that? Sharon, maybe all of you in the newsroom can see better when Ian zooms in, but it looks to me like they may have found something."

"Yes, Darcy. I can see here on my monitor. The forensics team is bagging evidence. As they move the firewood, they are being extremely careful not to disturb anything that may be beneath it."

"Yes, that's right, Sharon," the anchor confirmed.

"How does seeing this make you feel?" I looked up to see a small, bald man standing with his fingers interlaced behind his back. He smiled.

"I don't know. At first, I didn't want to see this stuff, but now I guess I kind of feel out of control if I don't know where he is or if he's been caught."

"I see. And what will change if they find something here."

"I don't know. Maybe they'll find clues that will tell them more about him."

"And, how does that affect you, right now?"

"I guess I think that if they find clues, they'll get closer to finding him. And I won't have to be so scared."

"I understand. That was very scary for you."

"Uh-huh."

"You are a very brave. It took a lot of strength and courage to endure what you went through and to get out alive. Do you know that?"

"I guess."

"I didn't introduce myself. I'm Dr. Mertz, Clinical Psychiatrist with the police department." He held his hand out as he used the other to scoot a chair up to my bed. I took his hand reluctantly, and shook it.

"Don't worry. I'm not here to make you uncomfortable. I'm here to help you work through some of these issues. But not only that, I am hopeful that I can bring some of your memories to the surface to help identify and find your kidnapper. But, Josie, if at any time you are done talking or don't want to answer something, please tell me. You are running the show. I will look to you to determine whether it's okay to move forward. Is that okay with you?"

"Yeah, that's okay."

"Was there anything about your captor that struck you as odd? Think of his hair, his smell, and his mannerisms. Anything at all?"

"He had crazy eyes. I remember when I first saw him, he smiled and called out to me, but he never made eye contact. Then, I got a chance to break free and I ran, but he caught up with me. I looked into his eyes and there was nothing behind them. I've never seen anything like it before. That's the only time I ever really saw him because when I was held at the cabin, I was in a dark cement room and the light was off most of the time. All I could see when he would come in was his silhouette."

"That's very good. Very good information, indeed. Now, you've been talking without taking a breath. I can tell this is difficult for you and I don't want to upset you, so we're going to change directions. Are you sleeping okay?"

"I was until last night. I woke up full of sweat in the middle of the night."

"Okay, that is your body's response to stress. You've been through a really traumatic event, and your body and mind need to heal. Part of the healing process is to talk with someone to help work through the events. I have several names of people you can meet with after you leave the hospital." He leaned over to give my mom a list of names.

"Thank you, Doctor. Do you take patients?"

"I'm sorry, but no. I work solely for the police department to help assess a victim before they are released from the hospital, and sometimes work with them to recall details or work with a sketch artist. I may meet with you again, if any other memories surface, but the doctor of your choosing will contact me if that occurs. In the meantime, as soon as the doctor determines you are on the mend, you'll be taken to a safe house where you can meet with someone from that list."

"Okay. Thank you." I managed to say.

He stood to leave and added, "It's vital to your future that you talk with one of them. Be as open to the process as possible, Josie. It will help."

"What about Jason? Have you talked to him?"

"I have not. The doctors aren't ready for him to talk yet."

"Do you know if he's doing okay?"

"You care about him, don't you."

"It wasn't his fault. I don't want him to get in trouble. He tried to save me."

"I know that." He patted his jacket pocket, pulling out a set of keys before adding, "The police know that, too. What he did, he did to survive. He's not going to get into trouble. He's a victim, too." He looked at me with kindness in his heart and gave a smile before heading out.

"Wait. Do you think he'll ever talk to me again?"

"I'm sure he will, Josie. But you both have a lot of healing to do. You are going to have a rollercoaster of emotions. It's completely normal to experience anger, hatred, sadness, fear, and all the other emotions that go with a traumatic experience. You may think you are ready for a friendship right now, but you need to take time for yourself. And he needs to take time for himself. I have no doubt that you will get through this. But don't rush it."

"Thanks."

"You bet."

33

The rest of the afternoon passed slowly. The police presence was much heavier than the night before. Eric had called three times, and Em got on the phone. She squealed when I talked to her. It felt so good to hear her voice. I missed her so much. I managed to fall asleep for a while and woke to the nurse changing my antibiotic IV bag.

"Hi, there, sweetheart. I'm the new shift nurse. You can call me Carrie," she said, as she turned my wrist over in her hands, checking the bandage. Peeling back the end, she peeked underneath. "That's looking much better than your first night here."

"You were my nurse? I don't remember meeting you."

"We had you on some pretty strong drugs that night. I wouldn't expect you to remember me," she smiled.

She was a tall, blonde woman with a kind, gentle way about her. Her smile was familiar. Instantly feeling comfortable with her, I took the opportunity to ask her about the latest news.

"Did they find anything? At the cabin, I mean."

"Sweetie, I don't know if I should be talking to you about this. Would you like me to call one of the officers in here?"

"No, no. Please, don't. I just want to know what's going on, but I don't feel very comfortable with the policemen out there. Maybe if there was a girl police officer out there, but there's not. The only girl detective I've seen has left."

"Well, I suppose you could turn on the news and see it anyway..." She bit her lip, thinking a moment before continuing. "There was a press conference. The Chief of Police reported that they did find some evidence." She placed her hand over mine.

"Like what?"

"They found some clothing and jewelry. And they are sifting through some remains to see if there is a link to that Chuck Butler guy."

"Remains—you mean a body?"

"Yes. Honey, I really think I should have the officer talk to you about this."

As Mom stirred I decided to end the conversation. "No, that's okay. Really. That's all I wanted to know."

As soon as she left, I turned the TV on. Mom opened her eyes and stretched. "How are you feeling?" She walked over and kissed my forehead. "I think your fever is gone," she smiled.

As I flipped through the channels searching for news, Mom stared at me.

"What?"

"Josie, what are you doing? Do you think this is healthy? I really think it's best to remove the news stories for now."

"Mom, it's the only sense of control I feel right now."

I didn't find any news reports talking about the search. "Did you hear anything?"

Mom sighed.

"Mom, if you know something, you have to tell me. Don't you think it would be better for me to hear it from you?" Using her emotions had always been my go-to method.

"Okay. They found some evidence. They are going through it right now, but they did find the remains of what appears to be a man and two girls."

"Three people? Wow. The boy I was with told me there were other girls, but he didn't know what happened to them. But there were three girls before me. What about the third?"

"I don't know. I think they are still processing the scene. A lot was damaged in the fire. Most of the evidence they found came from the grounds surrounding the cabin."

"Do you think they'll find these guys?"

"I hope so, Josie. It's bigger than just Jim and the man who took you. There's a big network of people involved." Tears formed in her eyes as she realized what I had been through. "They also found tapes among the rubble. They are trying to recover recordings that might be salvageable."

"Mom, I'm going to be okay. I'm determined to get through this and get back to normal. With you, and Eric, and Em by my side, I'll be okay.

COMING SOON!

A DETERMINED MIND

Continue Reading for

an Excerpt from Book 2...

1

It was 2 o'clock in the morning when I heard the noise at my window. Freezing in my bed, I held my breath. It had been three years since I was taken. Life hadn't been the same, although I tried to go back to "normal". Wishing to regain thoughts, memories, and dreams of my own, I failed as my mind went to that dark cell in which I remained for over six weeks three years earlier.

I wasn't the same "me" I had been before that fateful day when I was taken and held against my will. I pulled strength from within over the last several years, knowing I had what it took to get through this. I wanted a normal life and I was determined to have it. That is what I told myself. It helped, sometimes, though I still got jumpy.

I heard it again. I crawled from my safe, warm bed, slinking down to the floor, in fear that I was casting shadows on the wall, alerting my abductor that I was, in fact, in the room. I hadn't slept with the light off since I returned home. The memories were too fresh. Mom and Eric were protective of me, rightfully so. But I resented it. In the household, things were good. Mom and Eric stopped fighting, and Eric was holding down a job, even getting a promotion. Em was as sweet as ever, and the only one who didn't treat me differently, including my friends. Regardless of things being better in the home, I couldn't stand my parents' sad looks. The words "Are you okay?" rang in my ears far too often. Counseling was nothing other than a way for me to get away from the pity that crossed everyone's features.

As I slunk up to the window, carefully spying so I couldn't be seen from the outside, a crash came from overhead.

Scared out of my wits, I rose to find myself dripping water from the overturned fish tank Knuckles, my new cat, tipped over.

I grabbed Knuckles and started laughing, ruffling his fur as I recalled how silly I was being. In less than a second, Mom and Eric were through my door. Seeing my drenched body before her, my mom was stunned.

"What happened?" Grabbing a towel out of the nearest laundry basket, she covered me and managed to scoop Flipper up and toss him back in the bowl.

"I guess Knuckles was playing, and I thought it was someone at the window, so I crawled over here and—"

"—someone at the window?" she interrupted as she leapt across my room to look out, shielding her eyes from the glare on the windowpane.

"No, Mom, I thought that's what it was, but it was just Knuckles on the attack."

"And if someone were out there, they are gone now," Eric chuckled, trying to lighten the mood. "Nothin' is getting in or out of this house with good old Centurion Security watching."

"Seriously, Mom, I'm fine. I just need a shower."

"Ok, I haven't finished folding the laundry from yesterday, so those towels in the hallway basket are clean."

"Ok, thanks," I said, as I left her sopping up the water on my carpet.

We had moved from our last house. Mom and Eric couldn't manage to move forward with the demons keeping them up at night. Jim, my biological father, one of the people behind my abduction nearly three years earlier, had not been caught. We all figured it was best if we could start fresh.

My only complaint was that I had my own room now. I always loved rooming with Em. It was something that made us closer. It didn't really matter that we had our own rooms, though. At least three nights a week, Em would sneak in my room and crawl under the covers to cuddle with me.

The water felt good after being doused with cold fish-water. I let the warmth cascade down my back as I piled shampoo suds onto my scalp.

Moments later, I got out of the shower and wrapped a warm, plush towel around my shoulders.

Shivering, I had an ill feeling deep in my bones. I hadn't had this feeling since the abduction. I'm 16 now—I've changed my name to

Josie McIntosh, taking my step-dad's last name. It's not a legal change because they can't find my biological dad to relinquish his rights. Apparently, the fact that he had me abducted isn't enough proof to strip him of his rights. He would apparently deserve a fair trial, if he could only be found.

I got my license and am looking for a job. Mom isn't ready to let me go. She says she lost two months of her life with me. I get that...I really do, but I need some space.

As I pull a pair of pajama pants and a purple tank out of my dresser, I flip the TV on. As I stare at the screen, the news anchor is reporting on a local girl gone missing. That sick feeling I felt after my shower—there's definitely

something to be said for gut instinct.

2

The missing girl is 12 years old—just a year younger than I was when I went missing. She's pretty...and young, I thought to myself with heaviness in my gut. Within minutes, my cell rang. Before looking at it, I knew it was Jason.

Jason Carmichael, was the boy I knew originally as Mason. He had been abducted years earlier by the same man who kidnapped me. He helped me escaped from our captor and we were rescued together after a long, difficult trek through the woods. We had kept in touch, and although we both handled things differently, there was no one in the world that understood what we had been through better than each other.

"Jo?" I heard as I picked up.

"Yeah, I saw it, too."

"She's 12. She's pretty. She's just his type," he said before adding, "I have a really bad feeling about this."

"I do, too. But why would either of them stay here? They'd have to be stupid to come out of hiding, you know?" I said trying to convince myself.

As he spoke, my mind wandered while I half listened to both him and the news anchor, my eyes glued to the screen.

Visions of my captor's greasy fingers as he touched my body... the men forcing themselves on me and hearing their loud grunts, while my body trembled... flashes of the dungeon where he kept me handcuffed to the floor... the way he used humiliation to break me... having to use a milk jug as a toilet... seeing Mason's back for the first time, noting the years of torture he endured... recalling the words my "father" said: *I don't know you. I don't care about you. I never wanted you. I don't have any kids*... the truck with S-k-e-t D-l-v-ry on the side and ba–

"NOOO!" I screamed as the news ticker scrolled

by with these same letters. I turned up the volume to hear the anchor describe a truck that was seen in the area when Callie Ashby went missing.

Mom came rushing in. "What? Josie, what's wrong?"

"Mom. He's—he's done it again!" I quivered with fear.

"Wha—" My mom's eyes widened as she caught a glimpse of the girl's photo on the screen. Her hand moved toward her mouth in fear.

"I didn't remember until now... I must have blocked it out. But, that's the truck he was in when he took me. I thought I imagined it. But those words! I can see them clearly! Some of it was blurred out. That's why they aren't listing all the letters. It must be a delivery truck— "*something* Delivery"—but it's the same one.

"I'll call Detective Falcor," Mom said darting out of the room. "This is big, Josie! You are remembering things!"

"Mom, I don't care about that. This girl— she's got to be petrified! Just tell him that it's the same guy."

I picked the cell phone back up and said, "Jason. It's him for sure. He's done it again. We can't let him do this to her."

Just then, Mom walked in and said, "I've got him on the phone. He says he'd like to go over everything with you. You up for that? He's meeting with the family now, but he will be here in the morning." I nodded before returning to my call with Jason...

If you would like to be notified when the next installment is released, please visit www.corinneleighdonovan.com, or email info@corinneleighdonovan.com and I'll add you to the mailing list!

Printed in Great Britain
by Amazon

75641454R00203